The Boy who be

The Boy who became King

Arup Kumar Dutta

Illustrated by
Viky Arya

Rupa & Co

Copyright © Arup Kumar Dutta 2004

Published 2004 by
Rupa & Co
7/16, Ansari Road, Daryaganj,
New Delhi 110 002

Sales Centres
Allahabad Bangalore Chandigarh
Chennai Hyderabad Jaipur Kathmandu
Kolkata Ludhiana Mumbai Pune

All rights reserved.
No part of this publication may be reproduced, stored in a retrieval system, or transmitted, in any form or by any means, electronic, mechanical, photocopying, recording or otherwise, without the prior permission of the publishers.

Editor
Mala Dayal

Typeset by
Astricks, New Delhi 110070

Printed in India by
Saurabh Printers Pvt. Ltd.,
A-16, Sector-IV,
Noida 201 301

Contents

Book One: The Younger Queen

1	The River Pearl	3
2	The Raft	12
3	The Younger Queen's Tale	24

Book Two: The Elder Queen

4	The Spy Sets Out	37
5	The Spy Arrives	47
6	The Spy Leaves	61

Book Three: The Prince

7	Growing Up	77
8	The Tournament	85
9	Escape	99
10	The Brahmin Prince	111

Book One
The Younger Queen

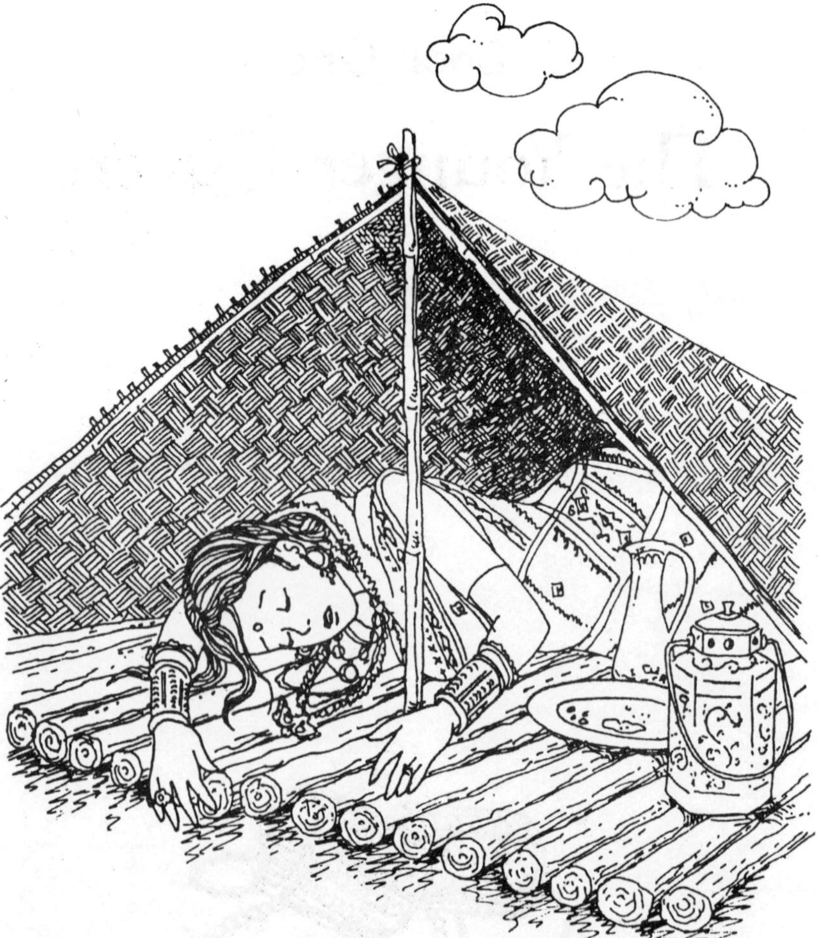

1

The Pearl River

The boys sat cross-legged on the ground, huddled around the fire. The old man, Kolakai, shifted the burning logs with a stick, causing sparks to fly.

The flames illuminated the faces of the boys and the old man's. Beyond the ring of light there was absolute darkness. Fireflies twinkled in the surrounding gloom.

A soft breeze, blowing from the Lohit river that flowed by the village, disturbed the curtain of mist covering the paddy fields and hutments. The boys moved closer to the fire, seeking its warmth.

Perhaps the breeze stirred the old man's memories. He suddenly spoke.

'This village wasn't always where it is now.' He paused and added, 'The Lohit wasn't always where it is now.'

The boys pricked up their ears. This had become a ritual. Whenever they could, at the fall of dusk, they would

The Boy who became King

hurry to join Kolakai in the courtyard of his hut, and sit silently till the old man began one of his innumerable tales.

Kolakai was a store-house of stories, some true, often imaginary, but always fascinating. It was from him that the boys had learned about the history of the region—how Sukapha, the Tai prince from Myanmar, had entered the valley of the Brahmaputra with a small band of sturdy men, defeated the various tribes, and established the Ahom kingdom; how his descendants, including the present king Tyaokhamti, had had to wage wars continuously to protect and extend the empire. The boys had never been to the Ahom capital, Charaideo, but so vividly had Kolakai described the city that they could visualize it in all its glory.

Kolakai was well past his prime. No one knew how old he was. He claimed to have been born towards the end of King Suteupha's reign. That would make him over a hundred years old which, obviously, was an exaggeration. He must have been in his late sixties. His skin was wrinkled, his features lined, but his eyes, now reflecting the fire-light, were as bright and sharp as ever. To the boys, with his flowing white hair and clear, strong voice, he appeared ageless. He loved children, and children adored him.

'Yes,' Kolakai continued, as if talking to himself. 'Our village formerly stood at a spot now in the middle of the river. The Lohit flowed much further away.'

'I've been told that our Lohit is also called the Brahmaputra,' Bashu, the son of Dhinai, the village blacksmith, said. 'Is that true, Kolakai?'

The Pearl River

'It certainly is,' said the old man. 'But only in the *Tantras* and the *Puranas*. We prefer to call it the Lohit.'

The other boys were getting impatient. 'The story, Kolakai, the story!' they urged. 'What happened? Why did the river change its course?'

'Well, the happenings that I am telling you about took place around four decades ago, when King Sukrangpha, the eldest brother of our monarch, was on the throne. I can recall the event as though it happened yesterday. Disaster struck on a dark, rainy night . . . the river shifted course and swept away the entire village.

'Fortunately, we were warned in time and shifted to a safer place with whatever possessions we could carry. Only one life was lost . . . that of the village no-good, Konmali. He was a wastrel who never did a day's work, so not many tears were shed at his death. The villagers took the calamity in their stride. It wasn't unusual for a rain-fed river to change its course, they said. It had happened before and it would happen again. They cut down the jungle, cleared land for cultivation and built the village anew.'

'Grandpa mentioned this incident once,' Nabin, a lively, short lad put in. 'He too said that our area was known for its floods.'

'Aha! But I know the real story. It was neither rain nor floods . . . it was the village black sheep, Konmali, who brought this devastation to our village. But Konmali had died and I did not wish to speak ill of the dead. So I kept quiet and let the villagers think what they wanted.'

The Boy who became King

'How is it that only you know?' queried Tipahi, a farmer's son, who always tried to pick holes in Kolakai's tales.

The old man looked heavenwards, rolled his eyes in mock despair, and raised his hands.

'Because I, Kolakai, see and hear everything,' he said in a thunderous voice. 'Do you dare doubt me?'

The boys were too awe-struck to question him further. With a twinkle in his eyes Kolakai resumed his tale.

'As I was saying Konmali was a wastrel. He had no land to till. He lived alone, eking out an existence doing odd jobs. But he was greedy. He dreamt of becoming rich. On the night the river was angry, he could not sleep. Water leaked through the thatch of the roof of his hut. The wind swept in through flimsy walls. Then, in the dead of the night, a powerful gust tore apart a bamboo window.

'Konmali sprang up. The wind was carrying sheets of rain into the hut. As he struggled to push the window back into its frame, his eyes were suddenly drawn to a strange glow coming from the direction of the river. Something was bobbing up and down on the water, emitting a fiery glow. The river seemed to be on fire!

'He may have been a ne'er-do-well, but Konmali was courageous. Picking up a *dao*, he came out to find out what had caused the mysterious glow.

'The elements raged around him. It was not a night for men or beasts to be out. Shrill, demonic shrieks filled the air. Ghostly shapes flitted around him, tugging at his flesh . . .'

The Pearl River

'But, Kolakai, there are no ghosts or demons,' Govinda, the village priest's son, interrupted. 'They are creations of our mind . . . my father says so.'

'He does, does he? Well, your father doesn't know anything! Creations of our mind, indeed! I can tell you stories of demons that will make your hair rise like the quills of a porcupine. I can narrate my experience with goblins and witches that will make your eyes pop out of your heads.'

The boys shivered, despite the warmth of the fire.

'As I was saying, fearful spirits pulled at Konmali's flesh. The sky was split by bolts of lightening and thunder. The wind howled in fury, but Konmali strode ahead. As he came near the river, he heard the tormented wail of a woman in pain.

"The Lohit was in spate. The water level had risen to the full height of the bank. The mysterious object from which the eerie glow came was floating in the middle of the river. The current was strong and the river was known to have whirlpools which could suck a man down to the bottom.

'But Konmali was undeterred. Leaving his *dao* on the bank, he dived into the river and swam towards the glowing object.

'It was a pearl, the size of a goose-egg. Everything about it was strange. It gave out a queer, bluish light. The swift flow of the river carried everything with it, including driftwood and clumps of reed, but the pearl remained stationary. And though solid and quite heavy, it floated on the water.

The Boy who became King

'All this should have made Konmali cautious. But greed had made him reckless. In front of him floated a priceless pearl waiting to be taken. It would make him rich beyond his wildest dreams. He grabbed the pearl, and swam back the way he had come.

'At once the river seemed to become angry. It was as if it was trying to prevent him from getting away. The savage waters swirled menacingly around him, trying to pull him down. The air was alive with strange sounds. The haunting wail grew louder and louder. But greed gave Konmali strength. With desperate strokes he crossed the river and reached the bank. There he received the shock of his life. His *dao* had vanished.'

Kolakai paused to fold a betelnut in a pan-leaf and put it into his mouth. The boys waited impatiently, while the old man chewed and then spitting the juice out, Kolakai resumed his tale.

'For the first time Konmali felt frightened. Fear lent him wings. He ran as he had never run before. On reaching his house, he paused to get his breath back, then examined the pearl. It, indeed, was a wondrous object, the likes of which few humans are privileged to see. Its blue rays lit up the interior of the hut. But the rays were as cool as water in winter and had a strange power—they had the power to soothe the mind.

'Wrapping the pearl in a piece of cloth, Konmali buried it in the earthen floor beneath his bed. Then, exhausted, he fell into a deep sleep. In his sleep he dreamt of the river.

The Pearl River

The waters were washing over him; his flesh was peeling away from his body leaving a skeleton.

'He awoke with a start. Panic-stricken shouts and cries for help reached his ears. Amidst the uproar he heard the sound of running water close by. He opened the door and cautiously stepped out. The sight that met his eyes brought his heart to his mouth.

'The river, which had previously been a long way off, was just a few footsteps away. It seemed alive, slithering like a python creeping upon its prey, as it moved closer and closer to Konmali's hut.'

The boys around the fire were silent. The flickering flames threw shifting shadows on their upturned faces.

'There was pandemonium in the village. Many of the huts near the river had been washed away. The frightened cries of men, women and children, and the mooing of cattle, created a deafening din. The villagers fled to safer areas. But Konmali stood rooted to the spot, paralysed with terror. His eyes were fixed on the vast sheet of water before him as it swallowed the earthen bank.

'I found him in that condition and tried to pull him away. He was like a mad man. "It's coming after me," he cried. "The river is coming after me!" He struggled with me like a drowning man. Although I am powerful as a bull, yet I found it difficult to hold him. So I hit him on the nape of his neck. He fell down unconscious and I dragged him to a safer spot.

'All the villagers had gathered there, and also the cattle.

The Boy who became King

Venomous snakes and wild beasts kept us company that night. We watched with horrified fascination as the river devoured hut after hut.

'After a while Konmali regained consciousness. He stood with us for sometime, then suddenly remembered that he had left the pearl behind. Greed drove him once again. The desire to become rich made him blind to reason. "My pearl, my pearl!" he shrieked. Before any of us could stop him, he snatched a flare from the hand of a villager and raced towards his hut.

'There was nothing we could do. The river had crept to the porch by then. He had just reached his hut, when the ground under it cracked apart. With a furious whooshing sound the hut toppled into the river, taking Konmali and the pearl with it.

'The river seemed to let out a sigh of satisfaction and was still. It shifted no further that night, nor later.'

Kolakai fell silent. His eyes were fixed upon the dying flames. No one uttered a word. No one moved.

At last Bashu broke the silence. 'It was the river's pearl, wasn't it, Kolakai?'

'Isn't it obvious, silly!' Nobin exclaimed. 'Konmali stole the river's pearl and hid it inside his hut. The river came and took it back.'

'I had rather be poor than go to the river at night,' a boy named Maulang said with a shiver.

'You have a wonderful imagination, Kolakai,' scoffed Tipahi. 'Now tell me . . . Konmali lived alone. He died

The Pearl River

before he could tell a soul how he acquired the pearl. So how is it that you know all about it?'

'Ha, ha,' Kolakai laughed. 'You're the only one who doubts me. I, Kolakai, know everything, hear everything, see everything. Little spirits come at night to tell me their secrets. But, if you don't believe me, look at the river on a stormy night. Perhaps you too will see a river pearl.'

'Heaven forbid!' cried Maulang with another shudder.

'You'd better go now,' Kolakai said. 'It's getting dark. Your parents will be worried. But take care. Creatures of the night will be on the prowl.'

'Look, a falling star!' Govinda suddenly yelled.

All the heads turned upwards. A fiery streak shot across the firmament and burnt out quickly.

'An omen!' Kolakai cried in a prophetic voice. 'Something unusual is surely going to happen in our village tonight.'

'Could it be a good omen?' Bashu asked nervously.

'I hope so. Have any of you seen a white raven lately? Or heard jackals howling in the daytime?'

'No,' the boys replied at once.

'In that case it could be a good omen. But it's getting late. You should go home now.'

The boys bid Kolakai goodbye and hurried home, worried by forebodings of disaster.

2

The Raft

Govinda and Bashu, who were neighbours, left together. They parted company at the latter's house, and Govinda continued on his way. No sooner had he entered his home than his mother, anxiously waiting, began to scold him.

'Where have you been? You should get home before dark.'

'We were with Kolakai. He told us a fantastic tale.'

'That old man is not good company for you. He puts silly ideas into your head!'

Her husband entered the room at that moment. 'Kolakai has a vivid imagination,' Govinda's father said. 'But he is a kind soul, always willing to help others.'

Surjya Bipra, the brahmin, was tall, and imposing, around forty-five years of age, with lean, sharply defined features and a hawkish nose. His eyes, set below bushy

The Raft

eyebrows, were clear and intelligent. His head was clean shaven like that of his son. A long tuft of hair, tied at the end in a bow-knot, hung at the back of his head. He wore a dhoti. The sacred thread ran across his bare chest.

'He's a heathen,' retorted his wife contemptuously. 'He doesn't worship our gods. He worships stones and trees.'

'To each his own form of worship,' the brahmin replied. 'There are many roads which lead to God. The scriptures tell us that God is in everything. If that be true, then He is in stones and trees and Kolakai is quite right in worshipping them.'

Govinda's mother was a simple, kindly woman, but orthodox in outlook. She often got into arguments with her husband because of his liberal views. She was, of course, always worsted in the argument. Now she tossed her head and retreated to the kitchen to prepare their evening meal.

Surjya Bipra placed a hand on Govinda's shoulder. 'Remember, son,' he said, 'all religions are essentially the same. The Ahoms who rule this country worship their God Somdeo. Their priests are called Deodhais. I have studied their form of worship and find little difference with ours. Their Lengdon is our Indra, Ja-Ching-Pha is Saraswati.'

'Is that so?' asked Govinda, interested.

'Yes. And the lessons which all religions teach are the same. Moral forces govern our lives. If we do good, we are rewarded. If we act in an evil manner, we are punished. Now say your prayers and eat your meal. Your mother must be waiting.'

The Boy who became King

After Govinda had taken a quick bath, father and son entered the prayer-room. Flowers were strewn at the feet of the deities. Plantain leaves contained the puja offerings. An earthen lamp, filled with mustard oil, lit the room. As they sat on the floor, the father intoned Sanskrit *slokas* and the son repeated them. After the prayer they prostrated themselves before the deities. Then the two of them went to the kitchen. The other children had already eaten and were asleep in their bedrooms. Surjya Bipra and Govinda sat on the floor on bamboo mats and ate the simple meal of rice and fish-curry served on a banana leaf.

The meal over, Govinda retired to the bedroom which he shared with four of his younger brothers. Here too a small, earthen lamp provided light. Govinda snuffed it out, lay down, and tried to sleep.

But sleep refused to come. Govinda's mind kept returning to Kolakai's tale about the pearl. The old man had made it sound as if the river was a living being and had wilfully destroyed the village to recover its pearl. But surely the river was only a body of flowing water, fed by mountain snow and rain, ending up in the vast sea! That was what his father had told him about rivers.

But then, just this evening, his father had spoken of something else too. What had he said? God was in rocks and trees! Then, perhaps, God was in the river too and gave it life! If we sin, we are punished. Why couldn't the river have destroyed Konmali, who had stolen its pearl?

Govinda was puzzled. There was so much he didn't

The Raft

know, about God and Nature and Man. He lay for a long time thinking before falling into an uneasy sleep.

He awoke suddenly. What had disturbed him? Could it have been a nightmare? He could not remember. On a distant tree an owl hooted. Kolakai would surely have found an omen in the bird's cry!

A gust of wind swept into the room. Govinda shivered. He was cold. His eyes went to the open window. So that was it! He had forgotten to shut the window. It was the draught of cold air which had woken him up.

Somewhat irritated, he climbed out of bed to close the window. The room faced the river. As he was about to remove the bamboo support that kept the window open, his gaze travelled towards the distant river.

Govinda froze. His heart seemed to stop beating.

There was a strange glow in the middle of the river. Some luminous object was bobbing up and down on the surface of the water. Had it not been for Kolakai's tale, Govinda might have thought nothing of the glow. But now the sight unnerved him. His eyes remained fixed on the light.

Gradually, the shock wore off and he began to think. Could it be the light from a fisherman's boat. But no fisherman in his right mind would choose that unearthly hour to go fishing. Moreover, had it been a moving boat, the light would have disappeared after a while.

Nor could it be a will-o'-the-wisp. Those mysterious balls of fire never wafted over water.

The Boy who became King

Then could it be a river pearl? But that, according to Kolakai, only appeared on wet and stormy nights. Tonight the sky was absolutely clear. The mist had not thickened into a fog to shut out the mysterious light.

His curiosity was aroused. He had to find out what was causing the glow. He wrapped a coarse-cotton shawl around his shoulders to ward off the cold and taking care not to wake up the others, he quietly unlatched the front door and slipped out of the house.

The dark, silent night lessened his enthusiasm. He balked at the thought of the lonely walk to the river-bank. He decided to contact Bashu. A companion would revive his faltering courage.

He ran swiftly to his best friend's house. Bashu was an only child who lived with his widower father. He slept in a side-room all by himself. Rousing him without disturbing the household would not be too difficult.

In those days thefts were unheard of in villages. Most of the villagers were farmers. Their wealth lay in their land. People did not lock up their huts because there was nothing to steal in them. There were no bolts to doors and windows. Doors were latched at night only to prevent wild animals which might stray in. But windows, too tiny for predators to climb through, were usually left unlatched.

When Govinda, on reaching Bashu's room, pulled at the window, it opened at once.

'Wake up, Bashu,' he hissed. 'It's me, Govinda.' He continued to whisper urgently till the sleeping figure awoke and sat up.

The Raft

'Who . . . who is it?' There was a trace of fear in his friend's voice.

'Me, Govinda. I've something to show you.'

Recognising the voice, Bashu came up to the window.

'What is it?' he asked, all sleep vanishing from his eyes.

'Do you have a *dao* in your room?'

'Yes. Why?'

'Get it and come out. There's a light on the river.'

'A light?' Bashu's voice quivered with excitement. 'Is it a pearl, Govinda?'

'No idea. But we must find out.'

'Do you think it's wise for us to go out in the night? What if it's a ghost or something?'

'Don't be silly! If you are not coming, I'll go alone.'

'Wait, wait. I'm coming.'

Soon Bashu joined him.

'What a dark night!' he exclaimed. 'I'm glad you're with me.'

'Look,' said Govinda, pointing towards the river. His friend saw the light and let out a startled gasp. Govinda caught him by the hand and pulled him along. They moved cautiously over the paddy fields that separated the village from the river. The crop having been harvested, the fields were bare.

The quiet of the night was only disturbed by the chirping of crickets. Fireflies twinkled in the dark. The boys skirted round a clump of tall bamboo, the leaves of which made an eerie, rustling sound.

Piercing howls suddenly broke out from the jungle that

The Boy who became King

fringed the paddy fields and grazing grounds. The boys stopped and looked around them fearfully. It was only the baying of jackals. Soon there was silence once more. The boys continued on their way.

As they approached the river, the light became brighter. The silhouettes around the glow grew more distinct. But the boys could not yet guess what it might be. A patch of sugar-cane momentarily hid the glow. Then, as they circled the cane-patch and emerged onto the bank, they saw it clearly.

It was a raft, but bigger than the ones the village boys made during the floods. It floated some thirty yards from the bank. The current was bringing it towards them. Half the raft was covered by a roof made of spliced bamboo. A lamp burned underneath this shelter. It had been the light from this lamp which had attracted their attention.

Bashu sighed, whether from relief or disappointment Govinda could not tell. 'It's only a raft,' Bashu whispered. 'I wish it had been a pearl! We've come all this way for nothing. And in the night too!'

'Wait,' Govinda said, restraining Bashu from turning back. 'There's something strange about this raft. It seems deserted, yet a lamp is burning inside.'

The boys waited as the raft came closer and closer.

'There's someone inside!' Bashu suddenly exclaimed.

'Yes. But he seems to be asleep.'

'Or dead!' Bashu whispered tensely.

'It will reach the bank soon. Then we'll find out.'

But, just a few yards from the bank, the raft got entangled

The Raft

in a clump of weeds. The boys had to go down to the edge of the water for a closer look.

It was indeed a big raft. Even from that distance they could see the intricate shape of the lamp burning on it. The flame was sheltered from the wind by a thin, metal chimney. Small holes in the chimney allowed light to filter through, lighting up the reclining form of a woman. Her face was in shadow, but the gold bangles on her arms and the diamond-studded necklace around her neck glittered in the lamp light.

'It's not a pearl at all, but a water-princess!' Bashu whispered frightened. 'Or perhaps a ghost in womanly form!'

'We'd better go and call our parents,' Govinda urged. 'If she's human, she seems to be in need of help.'

The two boys raced back to the village, repeatedly stumbling over the uneven paddy fields in their haste. On reaching Govinda's house, they woke up his parents and related how they had discovered the raft and the woman on it. Govinda's mother began to scold them for going out at night, but Surjya Bipra cut her short.

'We must go at once to this woman's help. I shall fetch Dhinai and Kolakai.'

A short while later the brahmin returned with the other two. Both carried lit flares in their hands. A hurried conversation, and they were off, the boys acting as guides.

On arriving at the river-bank, they found the raft just where the boys had seen it last. Kolakai and Dhinai waded up to it and, freeing it from the weeds, brought it to the bank. The light from the flares revealed the face of the raft's occupant—a woman of unsurpassed beauty. Precious ornaments adorned her limbs and neck. She wore clothes made of the finest silk. Her dress was embroidered with threads of gold.

'She's no ordinary woman,' Dhinai said in wonder. 'Only the nobility wear such fine dresses. And just look at her ornaments! They must be worth a fortune!'

Surjya Bipra touched the woman's cheeks. They were ice cold. He prised open the closed eyelids and examined her eyes.

'She's alive, but very weak. We'll have to carry her to the village.'

Dhinai and Kolakai set to work, cutting and splicing bamboo stems, and fashioning a make-shift stretcher. Then Kolakai lifted the woman and placed her gently on it. They quickly searched the raft for clues to the woman's identity, but found nothing. There were only traces of food and an empty, brass pitcher. The woman must have been on the raft for many days. The lamp as well as the chimney were made of plated gold, further proof that the woman was of high social standing.

The raft, built with logs lashed together with strands of cane, was finely crafted. 'It's not usual for a woman of her stature to travel on a raft,' the brahmin observed. 'She must be in great danger. If we leave the raft here, someone will surely discover it.'

'You're right,' Kolakai agreed. 'We must destroy it.'

They hacked at the lashings with their *daos*, dismantled the raft, and set the logs adrift. Soon all traces of the raft

The Raft

had vanished. Kolakai and Dhinai lifted the stretcher, while Surjya Bipra and the boys lit their way by holding aloft the flares. On reaching Surjya Bipra's house, they put the stretcher in the outer room.

At first the brahmin's wife was overawed by the sight of the strange woman dressed in such finery. Being superstitious, she was terrified that the men had brought an evil spirit into the household. But when she saw the woman was weak and pale, her natural kindness overcame her fear.

She bustled about, arranging for the stranger's comfort. A thick matting was fetched, and a cotton mattress laid upon it. Dhinai and Kolakai carefully shifted the woman from the stretcher onto this bed. The brahmin's wife wrapped her in a coarse-cotton shawl. She went to the kitchen and returned with a lighted *chula*. Spreading mustard oil on her palms, she warmed them at the fire and rubbed the warm oil on to the soles of the stranger's feet.

The feet were ice cold. She was still as death. It looked as if it would be impossible to revive the ill woman. Kolakai hurried home and brought back some medicinal herbs. After pounding the herbs into a pulp, the brahmin's wife applied it upon the woman's forehead.

The boys looked on anxiously.

At last, to everyone's relief, warmth returned to her limbs and colour reappeared on her cheeks. Her eyelids flickered open. She gazed at the faces around her, puzzled.

Bashu's father still carried a flare in one hand and a *dao* in the other. Seeing him, the woman cringed in terror.

'Please don't kill me!' she whimpered.

The Boy who became King

The brahmin's wife stroked her hair and face as if she were a child. 'Don't be afraid,' she soothed. 'We are your friends. You're safe with us.'

'Where am I?' the woman asked. Her voice was stronger. She no longer appeared to be afraid.

'You are in Kalabari village,' Kolakai said gently. 'It is on the north bank of the Lohit river.'

'Who are you? I can see that you are good people. You've done me no harm.'

'We are villagers,' Surjya Bipra replied. 'I'm the village priest. This is my house and the woman looking after you is my wife.'

'You were drifting in a raft when we found you,' Kolakai said. 'You'll tell us who you are, won't you?'

The woman closed her eyes and was silent for a while, as if deliberating within herself. Then she said, 'I'm the Younger Queen of King Tyaokhamti.'

There was a sudden hush in the room. Everyone appeared startled. They had correctly guessed that the stranger was of noble birth. But they had not imagined that she was a queen!

The flare dropped from Dhinai's hand. They all prostrated themselves before Her Majesty. The boys were thrilled. Not in their wildest dreams could they have visualized a queen in their midst!

'Arise,' the queen commanded. But the sweetness in her voice made it sound like a request. The men arose. The brahmin's wife remained seated by her side.

'I'm thirsty. Can you bring me some water, please?'

The Raft

The brahmin's wife immediately got up. 'We're poor people,' she said. 'We don't have utensils befitting a queen.'

The queen smiled gently. 'My sister, does it really matter whether the bowl I drink out of is made of gold or clay? All I ask is that the water be as pure as your heart.'

'Thank you, Your Majesty,' the brahmin's wife said gratefully. 'You must be hungry too. I'll make you a warm vegetable soup. I would have made meat-stew, but there's no meat in the house.'

The good woman brought water in a clay-pot and then went off to the kitchen to make the soup.

Kolakai asked, 'As far as I know, our king has two wives. The first is known as the Elder Queen. You must be the other one, Your Majesty.'

'I was the other one!' agreed the Younger Queen. 'But I'm a queen no longer. Let me eat first. Then I shall tell you my tragic story.'

3

The Younger Queen's Tale

After having finished the soup and regained some of her strength, the Younger Queen began her tale.

'My lord and husband,' she said, 'had married the Elder Queen many years ago. He soon discovered that she was a petty-minded, selfish woman, incapable of thinking about anyone but herself. His affection for her waned, but she continued to wield great influence over him. He took no decision without her consent.

'The Elder Queen was barren. If the king died without a male heir, there would be no one to succeed him to the throne. So, against the wishes of the Elder Queen but with the approval of his ministers, the king married again.'

The Younger Queen sighed and tears flowed down her cheeks as she recalled the events of the past.

'I was the unfortunate second wife. I come from a noble

The Younger Queen's Tale

family. When the proposal of marriage came from the king, my parents were very happy. So was I. Our wedding took place at the royal palace in the capital, Charaideo. The celebrations were marked by much pomp and gaiety.'

'Pardon me, Your Highness,' Dhinai interrupted. 'This happened just over a year ago, didn't it? The Lohit separates us from your part of the country, but we heard through cattle-traders that the king had married again. There was great rejoicing in the capital, they said.'

'Over a year ago!' the queen exclaimed in wonder. 'How time flies! It seems I was married just yesterday. The king loved me greatly. He showered me with costly gifts. I have a sweet voice and sing well. He spent hours in my company listening to my songs.

'The Elder Queen felt neglected. She became jealous of the affection the king showed towards me. She tried to poison my husband's mind against me, but without success. She slighted me at the least pretext, though I did nothing to provoke her. I felt sorry for her. I could understand and sympathise with her plight.

'But I did not imagine how vicious she really was. She wanted to destroy me, but was unable to do much as long as I was under my husband's protection.'

The queen paused and wiped away her tears. The men in the room nodded their heads in sympathy.

'When the Elder Queen came to know that I was carrying the king's child, she was furious. It was as if a knife had been driven into her heart. My maid told me that she neither ate nor slept for many days. My husband, on the other hand, was overjoyed. He summoned the royal astrologer to forecast the child's future.

'The astrologer killed a cock and observed its legs. "It will be a boy, Your Majesty," he predicted confidently. "He will bring great glory to the family's name." So happy was my husband that he rewarded the soothsayer lavishly. But the forecast infuriated the Elder Queen further. If the unborn child was indeed a boy, he would grow up to be the crown prince and I, would then be the senior queen, though junior to her in years.

'Yet there was nothing she could do. As long as the king was present, she could cause me no harm. She did make one attempt—she sent me a medicine through a servant. She had expressed concern at my health . . . I had been very happy that she had had a change of heart towards me. I would have taken the medicine, if only to express my gratitude to her. But my maid, who was as intelligent as she was loyal, threw away the potion, retaining the empty container. She told me that the so-called medicine would have destroyed the baby within me. She later paid for her loyalty with her life.'

'Cheeh!' exclaimed the brahmin's wife contemptuously. 'Can a human being be so vile?'

'Unsuccessful in this attempt, the Elder Queen now plotted to send the king away from the capital. A brother of my husband had been treacherously murdered by a neighbouring tribe. She egged on my lord, Tyaokhamti, to take revenge and wage war against that tribe, and lead his soldiers himself. The two senior ministers at the court, the

The Younger Queen's Tale

Buragohain and the Bargohain, were against a costly and meaningless war. I too tried to stop him from going, but the king was not to be dissuaded. He left the capital with a huge army.

'Ordinarily the ministers would have ruled the country in his absence. But his disagreement with them on the issue of going to war had made him suspicious of their loyalty. So, against his better judgement, he appointed the Elder Queen as Regent. This gave her unlimited authority. Even the Buragohain or the Bargohain did not dare defy her. The king had scarcely left than she framed false charges against me and ordered that I be beheaded.'

'You poor thing!' the brahmin's wife spoke not as a subject to her queen, but as one woman to another. 'How you've suffered.'

'A false, deceitful woman,' added Surjya Bipra, and the others nodded their heads in agreement.

'The nobles knew I was innocent,' continued the Younger Queen. 'But they feared her reprisals if they were to help me. I was thrown into a dungeon. Then, a few nights ago, the executioner came to my cell.

'I was determined to face death boldly. I knew I was innocent and that lent me strength. With a prayer on my lips, I walked out of my cell. It was a dark, moonless night, I remember. To my amazement the executioner did not take me to the place of public execution. He took a different route and a short while later we met the Buragohain with a group of men. They had been waiting for us.

'The senior minister bowed to me. "I have bribed the

executioner to let you go," he told me. "He will show the Elder Queen goat's blood on his blade to confirm that he has beheaded you. He will claim that your body has been fed to the jackals. Now come, there's no time to lose."

'I was put into a palanquin and our party moved through fields and jungles till we arrived at the Dihing river. A raft was waiting there with some food and water. "Farewell, Your Highness," my saviour called out. "May the gods protect you and your child!" His men pushed the raft and set it adrift.

'I have spent three days and nights on the raft, hiding under the shelter lest someone see me. I have been fortunate to have survived and fallen into the hands of good people like you.'

'You are in great danger, Your Majesty,' said Surjya Bipra. 'If the Elder Queen finds out that you have escaped, she'll leave no stone unturned to find you and kill you.'

'I'm not afraid for myself. I don't have much to live for. I've lost a husband, I'm queen no longer. But I have to live for the child within me. It must be protected.'

Dhinai lifted up his *dao*. His swarthy features were aglow with passion as he said, 'Your Highness, if the need arises, we'll lay down our lives for you.'

'Apart from those present in this room, no one knows of your arrival,' Kolakai said. 'You can be assured of our silence.'

'But the villagers will know,' pointed out the brahmin's wife. 'A stranger's presence in this small village will set tongues wagging.'

The Younger Queen's Tale

Kolakai had a suggestion. 'I live alone,' he said. 'My hut is isolated from the others. We can hide her there.'

'But for how long?' asked Dhinai. 'Someone's sure to find out one day or another.'

'You're right,' agreed Surjya Bipra. 'We have to be very careful.' Turning to the Younger Queen, he asked, 'Can you pretend to be a commoner for a while, Your Majesty?'

'I do not need to pretend,' the queen answered. 'I am a commoner now. Remember, I have ceased to be a queen. There's no need to address me as Your Majesty.'

'This is what we will do. I'll let it be known in the village that my wife's younger sister has come to live with us. She's from another village a long way off. No one will suspect anything.'

'A good idea,' Kolakai said approvingly.

'This young woman has just been widowed. She's also with child. There's no one to take care of her. So I've taken pity on her and had her brought to our household.'

'But she's so beautiful!' the brahmin's wife said. 'Her ways and speech are those of a queen. The villagers are no fools. One look at her and they'll suspect that she's no ordinary villager.'

'That can be taken care of,' Surjya Bipra assured them. 'We'll say she's just lost her husband and is in deep mourning. She has no wish to meet anyone. Her health is also not too good. I shall forbid visitors till she gets her physical and mental strength back.'

'An excellent plan,' Dhinai said. 'It might work. But

The Boy who became King

secrecy is essential. No one must breathe a word of this to anyone.'

Kolakai turned to Govinda and Bashu, who had been struck dumb by the Younger Queen's story. It was far stranger and more wonderful than any yarn spun by Kolakai.

'If the two of you speak of this to anyone, I'll skin you alive,' he warned.

'Our lips are sealed,' the boys promised.

The queen stood up with an effort. She took off her ornaments one by one and handed them to the brahmin's wife. 'Keep these well hidden,' she instructed. 'If someone discovers them, all will be lost.'

'We'll bury them deep inside the earth.'

The queen had taken off all her rings except one. Now, she pulled this off too and passed it on to the brahmin.

'Don't bury this. Guard it with your life, for it is the symbol of royalty. King Tyaokhamti gave it to me at our wedding. It has the royal symbol carved on it and only a king, his consort or his issue can wear it. If, someday, the need arises for my child to be identified to be of royal blood, show this ring.'

Then taking the brahmin's wife's arm for support she said, 'Come, sister, help me shed these costly garments. Then find me clothes suitable for the widow of a brahmin.'

The two women went to an inner room. Clutching the ring in his palm, Surjya Bipra thought deeply. Suddenly he hurried into the prayer room. Lifting the altar, he placed the ring under it and returned to the others.

A little later the queen, accompanied by the brahmin's

The Younger Queen's Tale

wife, re-entered the room. She looked quite different. She was dressed in white and wore no ornaments.

She looked so young and frail and innocent that the hearts of the men welled up with pity.

The ruse worked. The villagers had no reason to suspect that the new arrival at Surjya Bipra's house was not his wife's widowed sister. Her decision to remain secluded aroused no suspicion; they appreciated her desire to keep to herself. To lose her husband so young was, after all, a great calamity.

One man, however, was not taken in by the ploy— coarse, foul-mouthed Langi. Langi despised the villagers, somehow blaming them for the fact that he was poor and dressed in rags. The truth was that Langi was bone lazy, an idler, who took pleasure in creating mischief and spreading malicious gossip about the villagers.

Yet the villagers were kind to him. They tolerated his indolent ways, and malice and provided him with his basic needs. He often entered a household uninvited, and hung around till he was offered a meal. But kindness never evoked gratitude in him—he was as liable to curse and insult his benefactors as to abuse those who ill-treated him.

Langi was one of nature's oddities, clumsy and awkward. Though most of the village youngsters were terrified of him, some did occasionally taunt him and pelt fruits and stones at him. Mothers hushed their wailing infants by calling out his name. He was surrounded by an aura of superstition. People believed that seeing Langi the first thing in the morning was a bad omen—enough to ruin the entire day!

So Langi lived alone, away from village society. He partook of their charity, but gave nothing in return.

One morning, Langi entered the courtyard of Surjya Bipra's house in search of a meal and caught a glimpse of the widowed woman. Her beauty surprised him. She did not resemble the brahmin's wife at all. While being served food he talked to the wife about her sister. The woman's answers were evasive.

Langi began to have doubts about the mysterious stranger. The seeds of doubt in his mind soon grew into weeds of suspicion. There was something fishy about the woman! Not only had no one seen her face, no one in the village of Kalabari had seen her arrive. But Langi, being a sly fellow, was not one to share his secrets with anyone, unless it was for personal gain. So he kept his suspicions to himself.

The ill-fated queen, however, was not destined to live long. Her misfortunes had deprived her of the will to live. Separation from her beloved husband weighed heavily upon her. Day by day she wilted like a plucked flower. Surjya Bipra's children tried to cheer her up, but without success. His wife tried to revive her strength with nourishing soups, but to no avail.

One cold, wet, winter night, exactly a month after her arrival at the village of Kalabari, the Younger Queen gave

The Younger Queen's Tale

birth to a healthy male child. Later that night Surjya Bipra, Kolakai and Dhinai were summoned to the queen's bedside.

The Younger Queen lay on the bed, pale and weak, cradling the baby in her arms. 'My brothers,' she said, 'I feel the hand of death has come to take my soul away. Surjya Bipra, take this baby. Treat him like your own son. Call him Sureng, the name suggested by his father, King Tyaokhamti. May the gods look kindly upon him and you.'

The Younger Queen raised herself with an effort and handed the infant over to the brahmin. Then she fell back with a tired sigh, closed her eyes, and died.

In the span of a moment joy turned to grief. The brahmin's wife was inconsolable, and wept loud and long. Her young children, not understanding the cause of her grief, began to wail too.

Aroused by their heart-rending cries, the neighbours arrived and assembled in the courtyard. They helped carry the corpse to an open ground near a bamboo grove to cremate it. The Younger Queen had been brought on a stretcher to the village, Kolakai recalled. Now she was leaving it on another stretcher! The old man's eyes grew moist at the thought.

They built a funeral pyre of wood and Govinda set it alight. Surjya Bipra chanted prayers. The mourners waited with bowed heads as the flames consumed the Younger Queen's body. At last the flames died out. The villagers returned to their homes. Surjya Bipra, Kolakai and Dhinai remained behind at the cremation ground.

The Boy who became King

The brahmin had taken an earthen pot with him which he now began filling with the queen's ashes.

'What are you doing?' Dhinai asked.

'The Younger Queen was an Ahom,' Surjya Bipra replied. 'It would have been befitting for her to have been buried according to Ahom custom.'

'True,' agreed Kolakai. 'But we had no choice. She was supposed to be a brahmin widow. To have buried her would have given the game away.'

'We can bury her ashes, can't we?' Surjya Bipra said. 'That, at least, would be some consolation.'

The three men returned to the brahmin's house to dig up the ornaments which had been buried in the courtyard. Kolakai fetched a wooden chest from his home. They put the ashes and the ornaments inside the chest and bound it with strands of cane.

A fine drizzle was falling when they carried the chest into the jungle. Kolakai and Dhinai hacked out a tiny clearing and dug a deep hole. In it they placed the chest with the Younger Queen's remains and her jewellery.

They refilled the hole and piled earth upon it to create a *maidam*, a burial mound, as was customary among Ahom royalty. It was too small a mound to be deemed a full-fledged *maidam*. But, under the circumstances, it was the best they could do. Then, exhausted, they returned home.

None of them noticed the shadowy figure which had followed them from the cremation ground. Langi looked at their retreating backs and chuckled softly to himself.

Book Two
The Elder Queen

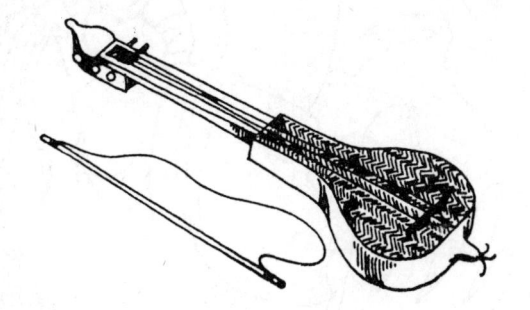

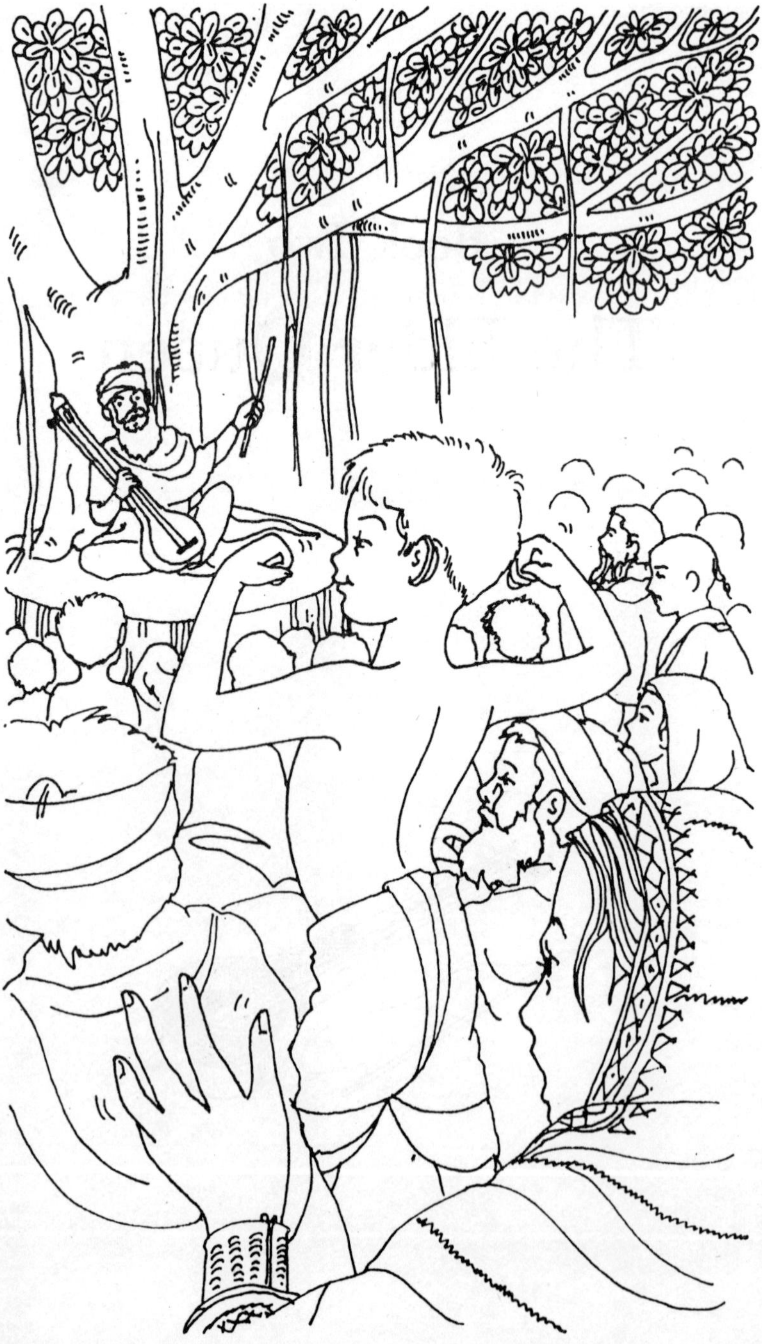

4

The Spy Sets Out

The city of Charaideo, the Ahom capital, was built by Sukapha, the first Ahom king, in AD 1243. Now, in the year AD 1388, it had lost none of its former glory, being a busy, sprawling metropolis, with fine buildings and smooth, unpaved roads.

The name Charaideo was derived from the Ahom words Che-rai-doi. 'Che' was town, 'rai' shining and 'doi' hill. So Charaideo meant the shining city beneath a hill. It was an apt name, for Charaideo was indeed a beautiful city, set in riverine terrain, amidst beautiful surroundings.

The royal palace with several acres of land attached to it, stood at the centre of the city. The walls and floor were of wood, and the roof was of closely woven strands of spliced bamboo. The palace had many different sections for the different royal functions, for instance there was a section where the king held discussions with his ministers on affairs of the realm, another where he accepted tribute from chieftains or petitions from his subjects, yet another for entertainment and so on. The sections were interconnected by passageways.

In an ante-room of the palace the Elder Queen of King Tyaokhamti reclined on a couch. Her chamber was luxuriously furnished. The draperies and linen were of the finest silk. The lamps, betelnut trays and bowls were made of gold or silver. Even the spittoon was plated with gold and inlaid with precious gems.

The Elder Queen's features were harsh and cold. She may have been beautiful once but now, with her stone-hard eyes and unyielding expression, she looked unattractive. Yet her manner was regal. She had a commanding presence which struck terror in the stoutest heart.

The fire of jealousy caused by her husband's remarriage had been doused long ago. Six years had passed since the Younger Queen had been beheaded. With her had died the unborn child. That moment, when the executioner had shown her his *dao* stained with the wretched woman's blood, had been the happiest in her life.

The Elder Queen's thin lips curved into a cruel smile as she recalled the events that had followed the execution. When her husband returned from the war, the Elder Queen told him of the treachery of the Younger Queen.

Weaving a web of lies, she told him that the Younger Queen had conspired with the ministers of the court to oust him from the throne. Had the Younger Queen not been beheaded, she would have been ruling the kingdom instead

The Spy Sets Out

of him. She bribed palace servants to corroborate her story. The king had been devastated. The Elder Queen wielded great influence over the weak monarch and turned him against the Younger Queen. The king's ministers, aware of her hold over the king, did not defend the Younger Queen and speak up for her.

The Elder Queen now had the king eating out of her hands. He consulted her on every thing. Yet, she neither felt safe nor had peace of mind. Danger surrounded her on all sides.

The ministers, especially the Buragohain and the Bargohain, were growing more defiant day by day. They were too powerful to be challenged. They had even dared rebuke the king for his folly in embarking on a needless and wasteful war. Their defiance was becoming intolerable. Something had to be done.

As she lay plotting and planning, a servant announced the arrival of the king. Moments later the king entered the ante-chamber. The Elder Queen hastily got up and touched his feet. The king motioned her to sit beside him.

Tyaokhamti was a tall, handsome man. He looked every inch a king. He had come directly from a conference with his ministers, and was dressed in his royal robes. The gems on his clothes glittered as he moved. Seeing his muscular body and bright face, one could not guess that he was, in fact, weak and wilful.

Taking off his diamond-studded headgear, he placed it on a low table, and sat down on the couch. The Elder Queen noticed the worried frown on his forehead.

The Boy who became King

'Is anything the matter, My Lord?' she asked anxiously.

'I've been quarrelling with my ministers again. They are becoming too arrogant. They presume to disagree with me on every little matter of the State. The Buragohain went too far today. He has served me with an ultimatum!'

'An ultimatum?'

'Yes. He asked me to choose between my ministers and you. "Who rules the kingdom?" he asked. "We or the Elder Queen?" He accused me of ignoring the collective wisdom of my court and threatened dire consequences.'

The queen's eyes narrowed. 'Destroy them, Your Majesty! You are the descendant of the gods. Invoke your divine sanction and squash them as you would a fly.'

'That's easier said than done,' the king replied peevishly. 'The ministers are united as never before. The people seem to be on their side. Following your advice, I have tried to strike terror into the hearts of my subjects. In the last six years thousands of people have been executed or imprisoned. Petty misdemeanours earn severe penalties. If I confront my ministers, the people will side with them.'

'The people, pah!' the Elder Queen sneered. 'The common rabble! The lickers of the dust we tread on! They are too cowed down to attempt rebellion. Terror, my dearest husband, is the most effective instrument of governance. Use it again and again to break down resistance.'

'But . . . ' the king began hesitatingly. The queen cut him short.

'Be firm, My Lord. Brook no interference. Prosperity leads to power, power gives strength. If any of your subjects

The Spy Sets Out

has become too prosperous, pull him down. Instil fear into the masses. Ensure that no one dares oppose you.'

The Elder Queen's face had set into an evil, wooden mask. Only her eyes glinted savagely. Looking into those eyes the king felt a thrill of fear pass through his body. Those beady eyes and bared fangs belonged to an animal of prey rather than to a human being!

'But the ministers can't be cowed down,' he said tamely.

'Oh, we must use cunning and guile with them. First, we shall pretend to agree with them. Then we shall set one against the other. They are strong because they are united by their common enmity towards us. We must pretend to value one while ignoring the other. Then, when they are divided, we'll pounce and destroy them.'

The king relaxed. The worried frown on his forehead vanished. His wife's strength of character had put steel into his own heart.

'You're right,' he said. 'I'll do as you advise. This evening a group of jugglers are putting on a show. The ministers will be there. I'll single out the Bargohain for special attention while ignoring the Buragohain.'

'Good. I'll also smile and talk graciously to the Bargohain. The Buragohain can sulk in his corner . . . '

The show that evening went off very well. Both the king and his consort favoured the Bargohain with their attention while pointedly ignoring the Buragohain. This was apparent to everyone present. The seeds of discord had been sowed.

The queen returned to her chamber after the performance. A servant informed her that the officer who handled

The Boy who became King

her affairs was waiting in an outer room and desired an appointment urgently. The queen nodded her consent and a tall, lean man was ushered into the room.

A close confidant of the Elder Queen, this officer had been a co-conspirator in the plot to destroy the Younger Queen. 'I bring dismal tidings, Your Highness,' he said. 'Can we discuss it in private?'

The queen dismissed her housemaids. The officer lowered his voice to a whisper.

'The Younger Queen is not dead, Your Majesty. I learnt of this a little while ago and came to warn you.'

An expression of shock and utter incredulity appeared on the Elder Queen's face.

'Not dead?' she hissed viciously. 'Impossible! The executioner showed me her blood!'

'It was a goat's blood that he showed you.'

'Quick. Give me the details. How do you know that the wretched woman is not dead?'

'This afternoon a man came to me . . . the executioner's younger brother! The executioner died two days ago. On his death-bed he made a confession.

'It appears that he had been suffering for quite some time from a lingering, incurable disease. He thought it was retribution for his work as royal executioner. "I've killed and maimed many," he told his brother. "The gods don't look kindly on the likes of me. I am being punished for my misdeeds." His end was very painful.'

'The confession, man, the confession!'

'I'm coming to that, Your Highness. "I've lived a vile

life," the executioner told his brother. "I have much to answer for. My only consolation is that I spared the Younger Queen's life. While most of the others I had been asked to execute were criminals, she was pure and innocent as a newborn babe.' His brother probed and prised out the details.

'It was the Buragohain's doing, Your Majesty. He bribed the executioner to spare the woman and show you a goat's blood. He then took her, put her on a raft and pushed it down the Dihing river.'

'Does this informer speak the truth? Why has he told you this? What is his motive?'

'Before telling me his secret the man extracted the promise of a reward. His motive was greed. I questioned him at length. I am certain he told the truth.'

'Has he been suitably rewarded?'

'Amply rewarded, Your Highness. He is now floating in a ditch, his throat slit from ear to ear.'

The Elder Queen's face had turned into an ugly mask. Her features seemed as if chiselled of marble, so hard and pale were they. Her eyes blazed with fury.

'Six years!' she exclaimed. 'Six long years to uncover the Buragohain's treachery! I shall confront the villain and fling my accusations at his face.'

'That wouldn't be wise. The king too will find out that the Younger Queen is alive. Knowing his love for her, he'll surely find her and bring her back to the royal palace.'

'You're right,' the queen conceded. 'We must see to it that this secret does not get to my husband's ears. But the woman must be traced and she and her child must be destroyed immediately.'

Suddenly the Elder Queen's expression changed. Before the officer's astonished eyes she seemed to grow soft and gentle.

'You've done me a great service,' she said in a low voice. 'I shall not forget your loyalty. Now I implore you to help me again. Wherever she is, find the woman and kill her. She is like a festering sore upon my heart.'

'Your humble servant has already decided on a course of action. I have brought a man with me . . . a spy. He sits in the outer room awaiting our orders. He will travel the length and breadth of the kingdom and find her wherever she is.'

'Fetch him.'

The officer left and returned immediately with the spy. The queen was taken aback. The man had the features of a saint. His flowing white hair and cherubic face gave him an air of distinction. He did not look like a spy at all.

He prostrated himself before the Elder Queen. She bid him rise and asked, 'Have you been told the nature of your mission?'

'Yes, Your Highness.'

'How do you plan to go about it?'

'I shall disguise myself as a wandering minstrel. That way I can travel wherever I wish without arousing suspicion. But the kingdom is vast. It might take me many months to find the woman's whereabouts.'

'Take as much time as you need, but find her. When you

The Spy Sets Out

are absolutely certain that she is the one you are looking for, kill her. She was with child when she escaped. If it's a boy, kill him too.'

'Forgive me, Your Majesty, but I think I should only try and find where she is. The woman may be surrounded by people who know her true identity. In trying to kill her, I may be killed myself. Then you will remain in the dark about where she's hiding.'

'He's right,' the officer put in. 'His job should be confined to getting the information to us. Having located her, we can send soldiers to finish her off.'

'Fine. Return with the information. Let me tell you how you can find her quicker. She was drifting on a raft, which couldn't have carried her very far. You'll travel by boat over the Dihing. Let the currents guide your boat once you reach the Lohit river. Do you follow me?'

'Yes, Your Highness.'

'Look for possible places where the raft may have got stuck. If the currents take your boat to the bank, disembark and scour the area. Be cunning in your questions. Don't arouse the least suspicion about your intentions.'

'I shall do as you order, Your Highness.'

'Then go. I wish you good hunting. If you accomplish your mission, you can ask for anything under the sun.'

The two men bowed and withdrew. For a long time after their departure, the Elder Queen sat as still as a statue, her mind in turmoil. Then she stood up, picked up a fruit-bowl, and flung it at the wall, as if this senseless act of violence could lessen the agony wracking her bosom.

The Boy who became King

The spy set off early the next morning, on a small, one-man boat. He really looked like the wandering minstrel he was disguised as. He was dressed in a coarse dhoti and a tattered cotton jacket. His turban too had patches and was dirty. He carried a *been*, a one-stringed musical instrument.

His white hair and angelic features gave him a deceptively saintly appearance. He rowed his boat midstream, and let the current carry him. When the current took him towards the bank he disembarked and travelled around the surrounding countryside, strumming his *been* and singing devotional songs. Sometimes he also sang martial songs celebrating the heroic deeds of the Ahom kings.

He scoured the countryside for many weeks, moving from village to village in search of the Younger Queen. Wherever he went his melodious voice won the hearts of the people and he never wanted for food and lodging. He also learnt a great deal about the people's feelings towards the monarch. They had little good to say about him, even less about the Elder Queen.

But there was no trace of the Younger Queen.

Three months later he reached the point where the Dihing joined the Lohit river. He had expected that the current would carry him along the south bank of the Lohit. But to his surprise, the free-flowing boat was swept across the waters towards the north bank.

A few days later the spy arrived at the village of Kalabari.

5

The Spy Arrives

The passage of years had not changed the village of Kalabari. Some people had died, others had been born. But life in the village continued in the same placid way as before.

Kalabari derived its name from the profusion of plantain trees in and around it. Translated, it meant the village of bananas. The fruit was abundant and of many varieties. The leaves and stem of the plantain tree were also used as items of food. Salt was scarce in those days. So *kala-khar*, made from the ashes of banana peel, was used by the villagers instead of salt.

Those were prosperous times and the needs of the villagers were few. Except in times of war, when some of the men were required to go to battle, not much happened to disturb their peaceful existence.

The farmers grew paddy, pulses, mustard, cotton and

The Boy who became King

sugar-cane. After the harvest had been reaped, it was stored in granaries to be used over the year. Rains were abundant and drought unknown. Occasionally swarms of locusts descended on the crops, causing famine, but this was rare. Earthquakes were more frequent and sometimes caused great damage. Folks believed that the tremors occurred when the gods were angry.

Rivers, streams and ponds teemed with fish and turtles. The villagers used nets and bamboo traps to catch fish. Meat was provided by the jungle fauna; wild boar and deer were plentiful. Wild ducks and geese, as well as numerous water-birds which roosted in the shallows, were trapped or hunted for food. The farmers bred cattle for ploughing as well as milk. Eating beef was not taboo, though only some of the villagers did so. Honey could be extracted from the hives of wild bees in the jungle.

Each household grew vegetables in their backyard. Children were often sent to the edge of the jungle to pick fern, edible shoots and herbal shrubs. The children sometimes also went by boat to the sand-dunes in the river to dig for turtle eggs, considered to be a delicacy. Apart from bananas, many other varieties of fruit-trees were abundant.

Like other villages in the Ahom realm, Kalabari was self-sufficient. A villager did not have to step out of his village to meet his needs. While farmers were in a majority, there were many who followed other professions. Surjya Bipra, the brahmin, performed religious ceremonies, and also taught the village children. Dhinai, the blacksmith,

The Spy Arrives

fashioned iron implements such as the scythe, hoe, spear and *dao*. His wares compared in quality to the best.

Haria, the potter, made enough clay pots to meet the needs of the village. Though brass utensils were not greatly used, yet there was an artisan at Kalabari named Baduli, who made pots and pans of brass. There were no professional breeders of silkworms. This was because almost every family had a farm where silkworms were bred and reared.

Chikon was a *Mukhi*, a manufacturer of lime. He gathered snails from ponds and paddy fields and burned their shells to extract the lime. Snail-lime, of a blackish colour, was very pungent. It was used as a medicine for leech-bites; the villagers also used it to flavour betelnut and pan. There was a cane and bamboo weaver, and a carpenter at Kalabari. Some of the rivers in Assam in those days yielded gold. The precious metal was extracted by straining the sand and silt deposited by some rivers. However, since not everyone was permitted to search for gold, and the villagers did not have much use for it, there was no goldsmith.

When ill, the inhabitants of Kalabari consulted the local *Bez* or medicine man. He was a venerable individual called Khenkham. He diagnosed diseases by examining the navel of his patient. He was not a trained doctor, and often prescribed talismans rather than medicines as a remedy. Sometimes he claimed the cause of a disease was that the sick person was possessed by a ghost. The remedy he prescribed was exorcism. Fortunately the villagers, being

The Boy who became King

close to nature, understood the curative properties of natural objects, and relied more upon their own knowledge of herbs than the medicine man in times of illness.

Every now and then traders would come in boats and barges to Kalabari to purchase the wares made by the villagers. They bought items such as sealing-wax and snail-lime, as also cattle. The Ahom kings minted coins in their own names, but these were insufficient in number to be used as currency while buying and selling. So the villagers used the barter system, trading their products with the goods brought by the merchants.

Thus life in Kalabari flowed on an even keel. No one was very rich, nor were too many weighed down by poverty. Children were born, grew up and got married. Sons followed their father's calling. No one desired this man's property, or that man's wealth. There were few quarrels. Nothing ruffled the calm of the village.

On the morning the minstrel-spy reached the bank of Kalabari, Surjya Bipra was teaching some children in an open space in front of his house. He taught them what he knew—some arithmetic, a little Sanskrit, instructive tales from the Mahabharata and Ramayana.

But only a few parents sent their offspring to Surjya Bipra to be educated. Most of the villagers preferred to send their children to graze the cattle. Some of the older boys and girls also helped their parents in their chores. The children themselves preferred to swim in the river, catch fish, play games or go on a hunt rather than spend hours reciting arithmetic tables. So many of them, sent to be

The Spy Arrives

taught by Surjya Bipra, played truant. No wonder then that there were not many pupils in the brahmin's class!

Amongst Surjya Bipra's students was his adopted son, Sureng, and Gopal, the youngest of his seven children. Sureng was six years old; Gopal, just six months younger. The two were close friends.

Sureng was a robust and handsome child. Tall for his age, he stood a head higher than his contemporaries, and was far stronger. To the few who knew the secret of his birth, his royal lineage was apparent in his features and the way he carried himself.

The brahmin and his wife loved the boy as if he were their own. After his mother's death, for almost a year, they had feared and worried that someone would discover who his parents really were. But with the passing years their fears had abated. The boy himself had no idea that he was of noble birth. He treated the brahmin couple as his parents, and considered their children his brothers and sisters.

Unfortunately, Sureng did not take his studies seriously. Kolakai had presented him with two weapons, a catapult and a bow and arrows set. He was keener on pursuing a weasel with them than learning his lessons. It was only at his foster father's insistence that he sat in class.

Gopal, on the other hand, was timid and earnest. He compensated for his lack of strength by a sharp mind. He had already learnt several chapters of the scriptures by heart and could recite them flawlessly.

Sureng too was very intelligent, but he put his intelligence to very different use. Surjya Bipra had once come

The Boy who became King

across a group of children playing. Sureng was the king, Gopal his prime minister. One of the group had taken the role of a bandit chief. He had been captured and brought to trial before the king.

Sureng, as the king, listened patiently to the bandit chief. Then, to everyone's surprise, he had set the bandit free. Surjya Bipra had listened quietly while the six-year-old boy gave his reasons for the acquittal.

The man had taken to banditry because he was poor and hungry, Sureng said. The ruler of the kingdom was at fault rather than he. Sureng, therefore, ordered that the bandit be set free and instead Gopal, his prime minister, responsible for running the kingdom, be thrown into the dungeon.

Surjya Bipra had been amazed at Sureng's wisdom!

That morning the brahmin, as usual, was teaching his pupils in front of his house. The boys were reciting the addition tables in a chorus, when a commotion some distance away distracted them. Soon a young girl, who had been helping her mother wash clothes at the river-bank, came running up like a whirlwind.

'A minstrel, a minstrel,' she shouted in a shrill voice. 'He's going to sing under the banyan tree.'

Lessons immediately abandoned, the children clamoured to be allowed to go to hear the minstrel. Ordinarily Surjya Bipra would not have given them permission. But strangers seldom came to the village, and, to tell the truth, he himself was curious to see and hear the man.

'You may go,' he said, dismissing the class.

The Spy Arrives

The students let out whoops of joy and raced towards the huge banyan tree that grew near the village community field. Their teacher followed at a more sedate pace. On reaching the spot he found a large crowd had already gathered there. More villagers were arriving by the minute. The women and children squatted on the ground in front, and the men stood at the rear.

Kolakai was amongst them—he wore his years lightly. While others of his age were stooped, his carriage was firm and erect and his eyes had retained their good humoured twinkle.

Govinda, Bashu, Tipahi, Nobin and Maulang stood with the others of their age. They had grown into fine young men. They were still good friends. Each had taken up his father's calling. Govinda was well versed in the scriptures; his father increasingly shifted responsibilities onto his shoulders. Bashu was apprenticed to his father and had become proficient in making iron tools. Tipahi's parents had died— he now worked in the fields with his elder brothers. Nobin, son of the potter, helped his father, while Maulang, the carpenter's son, was good at making things from wood.

Slightly away from the throng, all by himself, sat Langi. He was a solitary creature, who preferred his own company to that of the villagers. It was also doubtful whether the others would have welcomed him joining them. Langi's crafty eyes were fixed upon the minstrel. But occasionally his gaze flitted to faces in the gathering.

Surjya Bipra joined Kolakai, Dhinai, Baduli and others

The Boy who became King

and exchanged greetings with them. An air of expectancy hung over the gathering. The minstrel held up his hand for silence. The buzz of conversation ceased. He thrummed his *been* and began singing.

His eyes closed as if in prayer and, in a voice rich with emotion, the minstrel sang devotional songs. The words were simple. They celebrated nature's bounty and expressed gratitude to the gods for their generosity. The audience was enthralled.

After a while he broke into a local hymn that everyone was familiar with. The congregation clapped their hands and joined in the singing. Finally, with a few twangs of his *been*, the minstrel ended his performance.

An appreciative murmur broke out from the villagers. They asked the minstrel to sing some more and, in response to their request, the minstrel began a ballad celebrating the Ahom King Sukapha's adventures. It told of how that valiant warrior crossed the Patkai ranges marking the eastern boundary of the Brahmaputra Valley, vanquished the Nagas and other tribes, and established the Ahom kingdom. With the change of theme the minstrel's voice altered magically, growing strong and resonant.

In the middle of the recital, Sureng, who had been sitting in the front with the other youngsters, stood up abruptly. There was a look of wonder on his face. Oblivious of the others around him, he seemed to be gazing into the past. Then, suddenly he pulled himself to his full height, puffed out his chest and looked regal and intimidating.

Many in the gathering noticed the child's odd behaviour.

The Spy Arrives

Surjya Bipra became tense and anxious and Kolakai uttered an oath of apprehension under his breath. Fortunately the brahmin's wife was sitting near Sureng. She quickly pulled the child down onto her lap.

The villagers did not suspect anything out of the ordinary. They thought it was just childish whimsy. A few youngsters tittered with amusement. Surjya Bipra and Kolakai sighed with relief.

Among the crowd only Langi thought Sureng's behaviour unusual. Half-formed doubts which had been buried for a long time in his mind now resurfaced. He watched the minstrel closely.

The man's face betrayed no surprise. Nor did he seem annoyed by the disturbance caused by the child. He continued his recital. But he was perturbed. His mind was in a whirl. What a handsome child, so strong and with such a regal air. When he had puffed out his chest he looked imposing and majestic—he looked like a king!

Whose child was he? Was he really a villager's son? Had he reached the end of his quest?

Stealthily through half-shut eyes, the spy examined the boy. He must find out everything about this youngster. But he must be careful not to arouse any suspicions.

He ended his recital on a high note. The audience applauded enthusiastically and asked for more. But he said, 'Good friends, I've come a long way. I am very tired. Allow me to rest today and I'll entertain you to your heart's content tomorrow. Now I seek the hospitality of your village.'

The Boy who became King

The response was overwhelming. Every family wished to play host to him.

'How generous you are!' said the spy. 'Would you mind if I chose whose guest I shall be for the night?'

His request was readily granted. The spy looked at Langi sitting alone and said, 'I shall stay with him if he'll have me.'

Everyone was astonished. Some of the villagers, upset at the choice, protested. Langi, however, cackled with mirth. The villagers had rarely seen such a broad smile on his morose face.

Langi rose and walked up to the minstrel.

'My good sir,' he said loudly for all the villagers to hear. 'I shall be proud to have you stay with me. I live in a hovel, but I'll try and make you comfortable.'

The spy's choice had not been made without thought. The fact that Langi sat apart from the other villagers had been the reason he had been chosen. A good judge of character, the spy had rightly guessed that a loner like Langi would be his best source of information.

He went with Langi to his home—a rickety, stinking hut, little better than a cowshed. Even from a distance he could smell the stench. He knew he would find his stay unpleasant, but could not allow personal discomfort to dictate his choice.

To his amazement, as soon as they entered the hut, the look of delight vanished from Langi's face, and was replaced by a hard, sly one.

'Who are you?' asked his host. 'What's your reason for coming to our village?'

The Spy Arrives

The spy feigned bewilderment. 'I am what I am,' he replied tersely. 'A minstrel who wanders from place to place.'

'You can't fool me,' said Langi, spitting on the ground to express his disdain. 'Nothing escapes my eyes, no one can deceive me. Those stupid villagers mock me. But I know their closest secrets. Isn't that why you opted to spend the night with me?'

The spy said nothing. Langi took this to be an admission of guilt.

'I thought so,' he continued, fixing the spy with a foxy look. 'Don't think I didn't notice how you watched that boy Sureng. If it had just been curiosity, you wouldn't have been so furtive. So I said to myself, what's up with my friend, the saintly-looking, sweet-singing minstrel! Then, knowing well who I was—a dirty, foul-smelling, foul-mouthed fellow, you chose to stay with me. I'm not dumb, my good minstrel. Come, the truth.'

'You're clever,' conceded the spy at last. 'I'll be frank with you. I'm a spy on a mission. I need information.'

Langi laughed uproariously. 'So I was right,' he gloated. 'If I provide you with information, what will you give me in return?'

'If it's what I seek, you can ask for the stars and they'll be given to you. I work for the king himself.'

'It's something to do with that boy, Sureng, isn't it?'

'Maybe. I don't know yet. Now listen carefully. Has a strange woman at any time stayed in this village?'

'A long time ago?'

The Boy who became King

'Say, some six years back.'

Langi nodded. 'There indeed was one. But why do you want to know?'

The spy looked disbelievingly at Langi.

'Tell me all you know about her,' he pressed urgently.

'There's not much to tell. I saw her only once and that too was a mere glimpse. She claimed to be the widowed sister of Surjya Bipra's wife. He's the village brahmin. He was present at your performance.'

'But you've reasons to believe she wasn't?'

'Right. The villagers were taken in, but not I. She was a real beauty, the brahmin's wife is as plain as a pikestaff. They didn't resemble each other in the least. If she was her sister, I'm a minister at the court!'

Langi doubled up with laughter at his own joke.

'Oh, she was a mysterious figure alright,' he continued. 'No one saw her arrive at the village. Throughout her stay she remained indoors. Apart from the brahmin's family, not many people saw her face while she was alive.'

'She is dead, then?'

'Yes. She died a month after her arrival, after giving birth to a boy. That was her child you were observing so furtively.'

'Is that all? Doesn't amount to much. She could have been any woman... even a brahmin widow as she claimed.'

'Wait. That's not all. After the woman died they cremated her. Later the brahmin took a pot filled with her ashes. There were two others with him. They put the ashes in a

The Spy Arrives

wooden chest and buried it in the jungle. Then they built a small *maidam* at the spot.'

The spy's heart beat furiously. Now more than ever he was certain that he had arrived at the end of his search.

'You've seen her boy, Sureng,' said Langi as a clinching argument. 'What kind of name is that for a brahmin boy?'

The spy forced himself to speak calmly. 'You haven't shared your suspicions with any one else, have you?'

'Certainly not. Why should I? The villagers treat me like trash. They feed me, no doubt, but they've never shown me any respect or liking.'

'Good. Don't tell a soul about what I now tell you. If what I suspect is true, that was no ordinary woman. She, in fact, was the younger wife of our king!'

Langi was completely taken aback. He whistled with surprise.

'A terrible, wicked woman, was that younger queen,' the spy continued. 'She conspired against King Tyaokhamti but, mercifully, was exposed. The king ordered her to be executed. The elder wife took pity on her and sent her off in a raft. The king has since then relented. They've sent me to find out if either she or her child is alive and to bring them back with me.'

'A likely story!' Langi said. 'The Elder Queen wanting the younger one back! Who are you trying to fool?'

The spy guffawed. 'You don't make false claims, I see. Nothing, indeed, can deceive you. With that head of yours, they should make you the Buragohain! Yes, the Elder

The Boy who became King

Queen has sent me to unearth the Younger Queen's whereabouts so that she can be destroyed. But I have to be absolutely sure. A mistake could cost me my life. Tonight you'll take me to the spot where the ashes are buried. Perhaps the *maidam* will furnish a clue.'

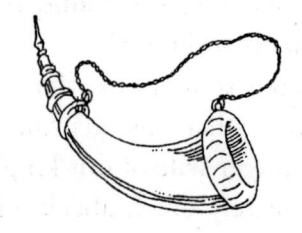

6

The Spy Leaves

Late that night, while the villagers slept, the spy and Langi made their way into the jungle. They carried flares, but took care to ensure that these were concealed.

On reaching the small mound under which the Younger Queen's ashes had been buried, they halted and stuck the flares in the ground. Fast-growing creepers and foliage had covered the *maidam*, making it difficult to distinguish it from the rest of the jungle. Had Langi not previously memorized the location, they might never have found it.

After clearing the vegetation with a *dao*, the spy used a spade to dig the soft earth. Soon the blade struck a solid object. Langi swept away the earth with his hands to reveal a rectangular, wooden chest.

The wood had rotted and the box crumbled as Langi prised apart the lid. But the ashes and ornaments were fairly well preserved. The spy picked up the necklace, wiped it to remove bits of earth, and examined it by the light of the flares. Time could not tarnish the precious stones. They glittered in the flare-light like stars on a clear night.

'Satisfied?' Langi asked.

The spy inspected the other ornaments carefully. Then after a pause, he replied, 'To some extent, yes. Such ornaments are only worn by ladies of noble birth. Perhaps the woman really was the Younger Queen.'

'Why perhaps? You sound doubtful.'

'There's one item missing. A ring... which only royalty is allowed to wear. It has the sovereign's seal engraved on it. That ring would have proved conclusively that the woman was the Younger Queen. There must be no room for doubt. I have to be absolutely certain.'

'The brahmin's wife must have kept it. Having seen such finery, she may not have been able to resist keeping one little piece.'

'That's most unlikely. Had she wanted, she could have kept the whole lot. No, the reason the ring is missing is obvious. It's the best evidence that the woman was the Younger Queen and her son the heir apparent. She would obviously have asked the brahmin to keep it at a safe place, easily accessible if it was ever required to identify Sureng as the son of King Tyaokhamti.'

'So the ring must be in Surjya Bipra's house?'

'I think so. It can't be anywhere else. I must have that ring. You'll have to help me.'

'Tell me, have I not been of service to you?'

'Yes, you have.'

The Spy Leaves

'I'll have to take great risks to acquire the ring. So I ask you again, what will be my reward?'

'Far beyond your wildest dreams. Find that ring and I'll take you to Charaideo and recommend to His Majesty that you be made an officer of the state.'

Langi beamed with delight. The spy's words were music to his ears. More than anything else he desired power that comes with authority. To the villagers he had always been an object of ridicule or pity. He would show them what Langi, the butt of their jokes, could achieve.

'Fine,' he said. 'I've a good idea where the ring could be. Tomorrow, while you keep the villagers entertained with your singing, I'll sneak into the brahmin's house and try and get the ring.'

The spy took out a small pouch from the folds of his dhoti and put the ornaments into it. The he lowered the empty wooden box into the hole, refilled the hole with earth and covered the earth with shrubs and creepers to hide all traces of their theft.

The two returned the way they had come. Langi shrewdly guessed that the spy would not give the ornaments to the Elder Queen. They were immensely valuable and the man was not so foolish as to hand them over.

But that was none of his business. The cold shining metal or the hard, glittering stones left him unmoved. What he had always desired was power. Now, by a stroke of fortune, power was within his reach. He slept peacefully that night and dreamt of Charaideo.

The following morning, while the minstrel kept the

villagers entertained with songs, Langi made his way stealthily to Surjya Bipra's house. The hut was deserted, the door open. Langi looked carefully around. Reassured that no one was nearby, he quickly darted through the front door.

Then without hesitating a moment, he moved on to the prayer room. He was certain that that was where the brahmin would hide the ring. His crafty eyes swept the room and then rested on the altar.

Without a thought for the sanctity attached to the wooden altar, Langi stepped up, lifted the altar a little, and probed with his hand. A jubilant cry escaped his lips as his fingers curled around the ring.

As he brought out the ring to examine it, he heard the sound of footsteps. Moments later Govinda burst into the room, eyes blazing.

The brahmin's eldest son had become suspicious at Langi's absence from the minstrel's recital. Being sharp, he too had observed the minstrel's surreptitious appraisal of Sureng the previous day. The minstrel had spent the night as Langi's guest. Now the host was not among the audience.

Govinda put two and two together and decided to go in search of Langi. By sheer luck he spotted the man. The furtive way in which Langi was moving deepened Govinda's suspicions. He followed Langi.

Though usually mild natured Govinda was overcome with rage when he saw what Langi was holding in his hand—the royal ring! Seeing red, he rushed at Langi, and lashed out with his foot.

The Spy Leaves

But Govinda had underestimated Langi. Startled, Langi dropped the ring, but he recovered at once and, displaying surprising agility, swerved to avoid the flaying foot. Govinda lost his balance. Before he could recover, his opponent grabbed the other foot and heaved. Govinda fell heavily on the floor. His head caught an edge of the altar and he lost consciousness.

Langi panicked. Not even waiting to pick up the ring, he ran out of the house as if he was being pursued by the devil, and raced as fast as he could towards the banyan tree.

The villagers, who had been listening to the minstrel with rapt attention, were taken aback by Langi's bursting upon them in such a manner. Ignoring everyone, Langi stumbled up to the spy and whispered in his ear.

'The ring is there. But the brahmin's son caught me red-handed trying to take it. I knocked him unconscious. When he recovers, hell will break loose. We must fly from here at once.'

The spy maintained his composure. 'Good people,' he said calmly to the villagers, 'my friend has brought me bad news. I shall have to leave immediately. But I'll be back in the afternoon. I beg your forgiveness.'

There was a murmur of disappointment. Many among the audience wondered what the news could be and how Langi was involved. But the minstrel did not linger to explain further. Accompanied by Langi, he set off briskly towards the river-bank where his boat was moored. The villagers reluctantly dispersed.

Meanwhile Govinda regained consciousness. Standing

up on unsteady legs, he shook his head to get rid of the dizziness.

Suddenly he remembered what had happened. Langi knew the secret concerning Sureng! He and the minstrel must be acting in collusion. The minstrel must be a spy!

They were sure to try and get away. There was no time to lose! Govinda ran as fast as his legs would carry him. Fear for Sureng's safety spurred him on. But he was too late. The minstrel had cut short his recital, the people were returning. The birds had flown!

He came across his father on the way. Kolakai, Dhinai and Bashu were with him. He quickly told them what had happened. They were very perturbed.

'They set out for the river,' Bashu cried. 'Come, you and I must go after them.'

The two set off in pursuit. On reaching the river-bank, they jumped onto one of the wooden boats tied there, and began rowing with all their might.

The Lohit was a vast river, with strong currents. The minstrel's boat was already well on its way—it was a small speck against the horizon. But the young lads were expert oarsmen. They too were familiar with that part of the river. The distance between the two boats narrowed.

The spy was worried. His was a one-man boat, now slowed down by an extra passenger. Langi was proving to be a burden. In the absence of room to wield another oar, all he was doing was standing near the stern, and urging the spy to row faster.

The pursuing boat was gaining on them—getting closer

The Spy Leaves

and closer. The spy grew alarmed. Their pursuers would be upon them any moment. There was only one solution.

Langi's back was towards him. The spy swung the oar in his hand and hit his companion hard. The powerful blow caught Langi unawares. He yelled in terror, tottered at the edge of the boat and fell into the swiftly flowing river.

Much lighter now, the spy's boat spurted forward and began to gather speed.

Govinda and Bashu were on the horns of a dilemma. They had seen the spy strike Langi and Langi fall. They knew that the unfortunate fellow would not be able to survive long in the cold, rapidly running water. Langi may have been a rogue, but they could not watch a man drown and not try to rescue him.

They slowed down their boat to search for Langi. Langi's head bobbed up to the surface once, his hands clawed the air, then the waters pulled him under for ever.

Precious time had been lost. The spy had far outstripped them. An hour later he was on the opposite bank. He then scampered up a slope, and vanished into the foliage.

Realizing that further pursuit was futile, the two young men turned their boat around. Surjya Bipra, Kolakai and Dhinai were awaiting their return anxiously.

When they learnt that Langi was dead and the spy had escaped, the men were dismayed. But there was nothing they could do. The spy would be well on his way to the Elder Queen with the information he had gathered. Only the gods could save Sureng now!

The Boy who became King

Eight grim-faced men had collected in a room. They spoke in low, conspiratorial tones.

The two principal ministers, the Buragohain and the Bargohain, were in the group. These two had carefully selected the other six, all lesser ministers of the court. Each had arrived secretly and alone.

There was good reason for their caution. The Elder Queen had posted spies everywhere. If she got wind of the meeting the consequences could be disastrous.

The Buragohain opened the discussion. 'We have gathered here for a common purpose,' he reminded them. 'We have to find a way to remove Tyaokhamti and his consort from the throne.'

'How?' one of the nobles asked.

'They must be killed,' the Bargohain replied flatly.

'Can't they be arrested and thrown into a dungeon?' a junior minister asked. The Buragohain looked closely at the speaker. But the man seemed to be speaking more from compassion than anything else.

'No,' he replied. 'A king alive is a constant source of danger to his successor.'

'But there is no successor!' another noble pointed out. 'The Elder Queen is barren, the Younger Queen dead. Perhaps it would be wiser to destroy the Elder Queen and let the king live. Regicide is a terrible thing.'

The Buragohain's mind went back to the events over six years ago. No one except the Bargohain shared the secret. Perhaps the Younger Queen had survived her ordeal and

The Spy Leaves

was alive with her child. But he could not yet reveal this to his fellow conspirators.

'It would be foolishness to spare the king,' he said decisively. 'No doubt the king's actions are dictated by his queen. He has been trying to drive a wedge between us, his ministers. He has also tried to cow down his people, but this has resulted in making them rebellious. In all this we see the hand of the Elder Queen.'

'The king is weak,' said the Bargohain. 'The country is going to rack and ruin. If we only kill the queen, the king might become more tyrannical. He might wreak vengeance on us. We can't take the risk.'

'True, true,' some of the ministers agreed. 'This despot and his evil companion must be destroyed.'

'Can I take it that we all agree on this?' asked the Buragohain.

The nobles nodded their heads one by one. Only one minister did not.

'I ask you again,' he said. 'Since the king will die without an heir, who will sit next on the throne at Charaideo?'

'The court ministers will rule till a suitable successor is found,' the Buragohain replied. 'The Ahom system of administration empowers us to do so.'

'In that case I too give my consent,' the noble said.

'Good. I and the Bargohain have set in order everything. We've arranged that the gates of the royal palace are manned by our men. A few of the king's personal guards might put up some resistance but not many will lay down their lives to protect the queen, I'm confident.'

The Boy who became King

'Remember, what we do is what we've been forced to do . . . stain our hands with royal blood to save the country,' the Bargohain said passionately.

All the eight men drew out their swords and brought the blades together. 'Death to the traitors!' they repeated one by one. 'Long live the Ahom kingdom!'

Before they left, one of the ministers had one last question. 'When do we strike?' he asked.

The Buragohain laughed a hollow, mirthless laugh. 'I have forgotten to tell you that, have I? We strike tonight!'

That same day, while the nobles were plotting the death of the royal couple, the spy reached Charaideo.

He was drooping with fatigue. Having been forced to abandon his boat at the Lohit, he had had to make his way to the capital on foot. Footsore and weary, he was sustained by greed. He had succeeded in obtaining what had been expected of him. The Elder Queen would surely be generous in her reward.

The spy hurried to the house of his mentor, the officer who had sent him off on his mission. The latter greeted him warmly and questioned him closely. He was effusive in his praise when he learnt that the spy had been successful in what he had been asked to do. The two set off together for the palace.

Dusk had fallen by the time they reached the palace. They were immediately struck by the tension in the air.

The Spy Leaves

The guards at the gate were unfamiliar. They looked at the officer and his companion insolently.

Moreover, the palace was usually a hive of activity at that time of day: servants would bustle about, royal guards stood in front of every door and passageway.

But today the corridors were deserted. No guards challenged them. They met a solitary housemaid who informed them that the queen had retired to her chamber and could not be disturbed. For some reason the girl seemed to be very agitated.

'Go and inform her that the minstrel is here with a valuable present,' the officer told the girl. She complied reluctantly. The queen summoned them immediately.

The woman was a ghost of her former self. The strain of waiting for the spy, coupled with a constant tussle with the ministers, had told upon her health. She was pale and haggard, her speech and movements were uncertain and slow. But she became animated when she heard the spy's news and the old hard glitter returned to her eyes.

'So the woman's dead!' she said harshly. 'But her son lives! You must leave this very night for Kalabari, officer. Take as many soldiers as you require. Bring his head back to me. I will not be fooled a second time.'

The officer bowed. 'Your wish is my command,' he said.

'Burn the village before you leave. Raze it to the ground. Wipe out the brahmin family. Those scoundrels must be punished for harbouring an enemy of the state.'

'It shall be done, Your Highness. But I'll need a formal order to show that I act at your bidding.'

The Boy who became King

'I shall give you the royal seal. My housemaid will bring it to you.'

The queen struck a small, brass gong. The sound echoed and re-echoed through the corridors.

As they waited for the maid to appear, the spy seized his opportunity and said, 'I look up to you, Your Majesty, to reward me for my labours.'

The queen signalled secretly to the officer, who nodded in response.

'You will be rewarded handsomely. My officer will see to it. But where is my housemaid? What's taking her so long?' She struck the gong again, but no one came.

'The girl shall be punished for her dilatoriness. Officer, find her and drag her in by her hair.'

The officer went out, but soon returned. His face had a puzzled and anxious frown.

'Something is very wrong, Your Highness. The palace appears to be totally deserted. All the servants, even the guards, seem to have disappeared.'

Suddenly there was a great commotion close by, cutting off the queen's response. They heard running feet, then the sound of a scuffle. A piercing, blood-curdling shriek rang out. The officer unsheathed his sword.

The door burst open and six men rushed into the room, with the principal ministers in the lead. The queen uncoiled like a spring from her reclining position. There was no trace of fear on her face. Her eyes blazed like twin flares. Standing ramrod straight, she said haughtily, 'How dare you enter my chamber without my permission?'

The Spy Leaves

The Buragohain laughed as he plunged his sword into her body. The queen uttered an agonised cry and fell bleeding onto the floor.

Her officer resisted, but the odds were loaded heavily against him. Struck a number of times, he too fell, blood spurting from the numerous stab wounds on his body.

The spy cringed at the assailants' feet, whimpering like a terrified beast. The nobles had no idea who he was, but his presence in the Elder Queen's private chambers was confirmation enough that he was in league with her. The Bargohain beheaded him with one slash of his sword.

Having accomplished their task the nobles, followed by their soldiers, left the palace to announce to the people that the hated king and his spouse were dead.

There was universal rejoicing. People lit bonfires and danced in the streets.

Heralds were sent all over the city. They beat drums and announced that the court ministers would rule the kingdom till a new king was selected. Dungeons were thrown open and the victims of the Elder Queen's wrath set free.

News of King Tyaokhamti's death reached Kalabari almost a month later. Surjya Bipra and the others heaved sighs of relief on learning that the Elder Queen too was dead. The threat to Sureng was finally over.

'It is the work of providence,' Surjya Bipra told Kolakai and Dhinai. 'I've always held that moral forces govern the

The Boy who became King

universe. Such wickedness could never go unpunished. Those who live by violence die by violence.'

'Maybe, maybe not,' retorted Kolakai, who had never been greatly impressed by Surjya Bipra's philosophy. 'What do we do with Sureng now? It is rumoured that the nobles are searching the kingdom for the Younger Queen and her child. Don't you think the time is ripe for us to divulge his secret and send him to Charaideo?'

'He's happy where he is,' Surjya Bipra, who loved the boy like his own son, said hastily. 'Who knows what dangers await him at Charaideo? Why should we knowingly push him into the tiger's den? Let's leave things as they are. Fate will take him where it will.'

'Wise words,' Dhinai agreed. 'There might be other claimants to the throne. Sureng is but a child. Sending him to Charaideo might be passing the death sentence on him.'

'Then let him remain,' Kolakai said. 'But I've a feeling he is destined to be king. I hope to live to see that day.'

Thus Sureng continued his stay at Kalabari, growing up with the other village youngsters. The six people who knew the secret of his birth kept it to themselves. The prince himself had no inkling of his origin. He was very attached to Surjya Bipra and his family and happy to be a brahmin's son.

Book Three
The Prince

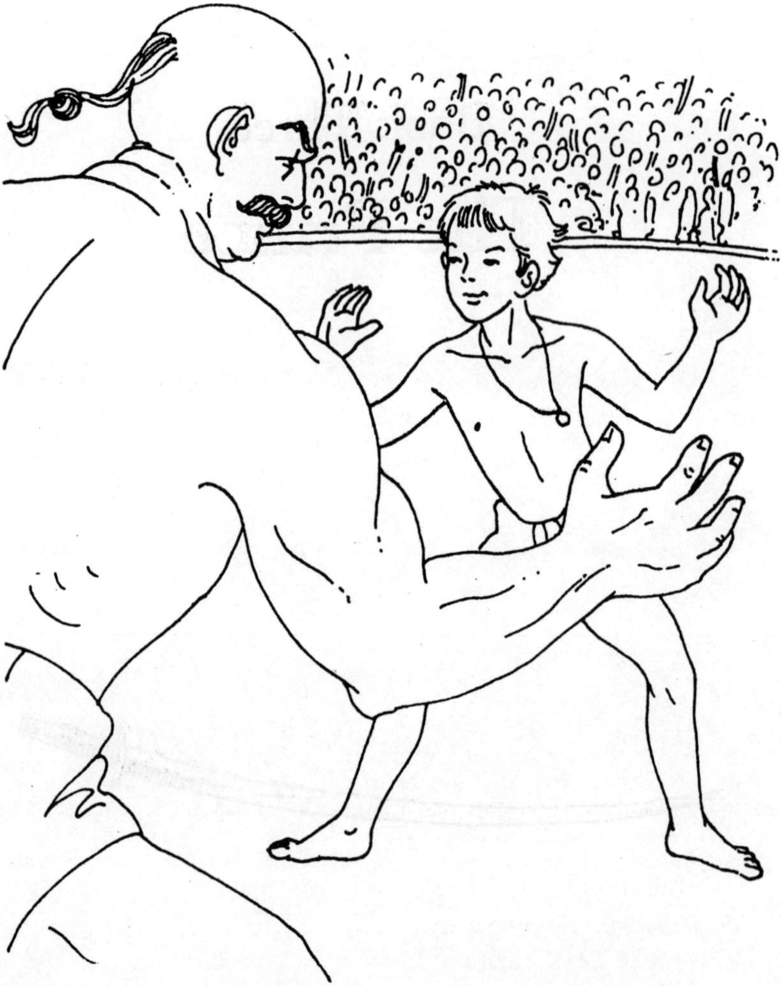

7

Growing Up

But Kolakai's hope of seeing Sureng as king was not fulfilled. Age finally overtook him and, one wet and dismal night, he died.

They buried him in the fields he loved so dearly. The entire village grieved for him. Govinda and his friends were inconsolable.

The years went by. Sureng, now fourteen years old, looked far more mature than his age. Strong as a bull, with a quick mind and wise beyond his years, he was a born leader. Not only the young lads of the village, but many of its older inhabitants, looked to him for guidance in a crisis.

But Surjya Bipra worried about Sureng's future. A few months after the king had been killed, soldiers had arrived in the village. They enquired if a stranger—a lady was living in the area. Not surprisingly, the villagers replied in the negative. The brahmin and the blacksmith knew why the soldiers had come. But they would never give Sureng away.

Surjya Bipra had hoped that Sureng would take up a profession and settle down. Having grown up as a brahmin's son, it would have been appropriate had he taken up a brahmin's vocation. But Sureng showed neither inclination towards the scriptures, nor aptitude for ritual. Surjya Bipra despaired of making a priest of his foster child.

Not that Sureng was a burden on the family. Thanks to him there was always fish or fowl at mealtimes. The boy was the finest of fishermen. He often stayed out late into the night scouring ponds and ditches with a flare in one hand and a *dao* in the other. Attracted by the light, the fish came up to the water's surface and were speared or hacked to death.

In archery he had no peer. He could hit a moving object with his eyes shut. It was said that he could cut off the wings of a dragonfly from a hundred feet away!

Whether it be in *dhopkhel*, a game played with a balled-up roll of cloth, or in a boat race, Sureng reigned supreme. He was an excellent hunter and used his bow and arrow with great skill to shoot down birds and game for food. He not only provided his family with fish and meat, but also with wild fruits and ferns. While most villagers hesitated to enter the jungle except in a group, Sureng went deep into the forest, often returning with his arms laden with wild papayas and other succulent fruits. He brought back enough honey to last them for years. The tallow extracted

Growing Up

from the honeycombs was used as fuel to light the earthen lamps.

No wonder that the brahmin's wife claimed that with Sureng's arrival Lakshmi, the goddess of prosperity, had entered the household!

The boy was completely fearless. He disliked setting traps to catch small animals, but did not mind if bigger carnivores such as tigers and leopards were killed by such means. He was adept at setting bow-traps and had killed half a dozen predators which were a menace to men and cattle.

Setting a bow-trap required careful observation and skill. A trail which an animal usually took had first to be located. The spoors were measured to determine its height, and a bow, fitted with a poison-tipped arrow, concealed at a suitable spot. A thin rope, attached to the trap, was stretched across the trail. When a tiger used the trail, its legs would trip against the rope, setting off the trap. The arrow would be released from the bow and would pierce the tiger's heart.

Sureng excelled in these and other physical activities. The villagers marvelled at his many accomplishments. A powerful swimmer, he would cross the mighty Lohit, even during the monsoons. His reputation as a wrestler had spread far and wide. The children of the village hero-worshipped him, while his companions acknowledged him as their undisputed leader.

Gopal, thin and spindly but clever, was his companion in all his adventures. The two were inseparable. Sureng was protective of his brother and any village boy who attempted to tease or bully him did so to his cost.

But Sureng's high spirits were a cause of concern to many in the village. Many mothers complained to the brahmin's wife about Sureng's escapades.

Finally one day three of the village elders approached Surjya Bipra and requested him to control Sureng. 'He's a fine lad,' one of them said. 'We all love him greatly. But he is the ringleader of the children and his antics are endangering the lives of other youngsters. Only the other day he dared my youngest son to swim across the Lohit with him. My son nearly drowned. To his credit, it was Sureng who brought him safely back to the bank.'

'My grandchild tells me that Sureng is bored with setting traps for tigers,' added another. 'He plans to catch and kill a tiger with net and spear. I told my grandchild that was risky . . . but the boy is adamant about going with Sureng.'

'You're right,' Surjya Bipra conceded. 'So far he has escaped unscathed but if he continues like this, he could come to grief some day.'

'He should settle down,' said an elder. 'He could chose his own line of work.'

'Oh, I've suggested it many times. You know Sureng has no interest in brahminical rituals. That's why he hasn't been initiated and given the sacred thread. Although we brahmins are not farmers, yet I have even asked him to clear forest land and cultivate it. But he despises manual labour.'

'We appreciate your problems,' said a villager. 'You should sympathise with ours. You must restrain him.'

Growing Up

'I'll do my best,' was all the assurance Surjya Bipra could give.

Yet he was perturbed. Sureng's recklessness could lead to trouble. The boy seemed restless of late, and was always seeking to prove himself in newer and more dangerous ways. He discussed the problem with Govinda, who agreed that the time had come for Sureng to get down to working for a living.

As they were debating the matter, they heard a commotion nearby. A procession of boys with Sureng at the head, a bow slung across his shoulders, was coming towards them. Behind Sureng two of the stronger boys carried the carcass of a big deer strung on a pole. The procession came right up to them and the deer was laid at their feet.

Sureng looked exhilarated! It had been his arrow that had brought the animal down.

'Tonight the villagers shall feast,' he told Surjya Bipra. 'We'll skin the animal and the flesh shall be sent to every household.'

The boys cheered wildly. Surjya Bipra smiled. It was impossible to be angry with Sureng.

Some of the boy's pleasure rubbed onto his foster father. How handsome Sureng looked! Just like a king! And, as always, how generous he was! He had killed the deer. By right it belonged to him. But the idea of not sharing the spoils had not entered his head.

Surjya Bipra and Govinda watched Sureng expertly skin the carcass. He cut the flesh into equal portions and sent his friends to deliver them to each household. Later, after

The Boy who became King

a hearty meal of venison, Surjya Bipra and Govinda called Sureng aside.

Placing an affectionate arm across the boy's shoulders, the brahmin said gravely, 'Son, in everyone's life there comes a time when a person must be prepared to take on the responsibilities of life. Childhood with its carefree days must be shed and training for the harsh realities of the adult world must begin. Such a time has come for you.'

'We're greatly concerned about your future,' added Govinda. 'How long can you lead this aimless life? Choose a vocation . . . learn a trade.'

'I'm filled with strange yearnings,' Sureng replied seriously. 'I can't understand them myself. It's as if I do not really belong to this village . . . that it's too small to hold me. I long for wider horizons, to step out into the world beyond.'

The two men exchanged glances. What they had always feared was coming to pass. The old man sighed.

'But where can you go, my son?' he asked.

'I have no idea. I'm restless. It's only my love for all of you that has prevented me from leaving Kalabari.'

'We understand, Sureng,' Govinda said hastily. 'I tell you what . . . there is the harvest festival in a few more weeks. I'll take you then to Charaideo where week-long festivities are held.'

Sureng's face brightened at this offer and his eyes shone with excitement.

'There's a tournament in Charaideo during the festivities, isn't there, brother? Kolakai used to tell us that they have elephant and buffalo fights and the like. Wrestling too, with the king giving prizes to the winners. Do you think they'll allow me to participate?'

'I don't know,' Govinda said laughing. 'Right now, however, there's no king on the throne. The ministers are ruling the kingdom. So the principle ministers will be presiding over the festivities.'

'Can Gopal go with us?'

'Sure. But I'll take you to the tournament on one condition. After our return, you must settle down and lead a more responsible life.'

'I can't promise anything just now,' Sureng replied in a teasing tone. 'I'll decide when we get back.'

Then, letting out a loud whoop, he ran off to spread the good news. Govinda smiled fondly as he looked at Sureng's retreating back. But Surjya Bipra looked sombre.

'The fledgeling has begun to spread his wings,' he said. 'Soon he will fly off and out of our reach.'

Unknown to his foster parents, Sureng had been giving some thought to his future. But he was confused. He was so different from the other boys. Many of them had shed their childish, carefree ways and were content carrying on their traditional calling. But such a life seemed too tame to Sureng. He could not imagine himself as a teacher or a blacksmith.

Yet what else could he do? For sometime now he had been feeling dissatisfied with his life. He seemed fit for nothing and yet nothing seemed fit for him.

He had often thought of running away. It was only his love for his family that held him back.

The Boy who became King

Sureng became more circumspect. Preparations for the harvest festival had begun. There would be a community feast on the eve of the festival, and many days of fun, games and trials of strength. There would be boat races between neighbouring villages and wrestling, archery and other competitions. The youth of Kalabari was busy preparing for these activities.

But this year the Kalabari team would be handicapped by the absence of its star performer, Sureng. It was he who had helped Kalabari win the over-all championship for two years running. Team-members begged Sureng to stay and participate, but Sureng had set his heart on meeting the greater challenge in far away Charaideo.

So, while the others practised feverishly, Sureng and Gopal helped Govinda prepare a boat for the trip. They chose one of the bigger boats which could accommodate three people, and stocked it with dried, salted venison and rice. A fishing net, *daos* and spears were also put on board.

They would be away for almost a week, travelling by day, sleeping in the boat at night. They had enough provisions for the trip, but would live off the land if the need arose.

The festival-eve finally arrived. The villagers feasted and made merry. They sang and danced late into the night. The next morning Govinda, Sureng and Gopal set off in their boat for Charaideo. Their friends watched them leave from the river-bank, and waved in farewell till the three were out of sight.

8

The Tournament

After crossing the Lohit, they rowed up the Dikhow which flowed past the city of Charaideo. The tournament was scheduled to be held on the fourth day of the festival. They had enough time; there was no need to hurry.

As they glided over the water they gazed at the countryside. It was mostly jungle. Sometimes they saw wild animals on the banks. Occasionally they passed villages, set amidst paddy fields. The mud-plastered walls and thatched roofs reminded them of Kalabari.

Other boats with people on their way to the festivities, soon joined them. They arrived at their destination on the third day.

That section of the river appeared to be a solid mass of boats. There were hundreds of them, so close together that one could cross half the river by stepping from one to

The Boy who became King

another. Govinda succeeded with great difficulty in mooring their boat close to the bank.

Having spent the night on the boat, early next morning, dressed in fresh dhotis, with *gamochas* tied around their waists and heads, the trio set out on foot for Charaideo.

Sureng's heart began to thud with excitement as they approached the city. He had never visited Charaideo before . . . yet, strangely he felt as if he was coming home. He could not understand why he felt the way he did.

The city was in a festive mood. There were sounds of laughter and music all around. Young children, dressed in their best, hopped and skipped down the streets.

They passed the royal palace. Although it was unoccupied, the ministers had ensured that the building and gardens were well looked after.

Crossing the market-place, the exotic goods on offer tempted them, but Govinda said, 'We'll look at these things later. We must reach the tournament ground early if we're to find good seats.'

The open ground in which the tournament was to be held was located beyond the main city. There was no need to ask for directions; a constant stream of people was moving towards it.

A fair had sprung up near the tournament ground. The traders were doing brisk business and there was much pushing and jostling. The boys craned their necks to see every thing around them. The shrill cries of vendors shouting out their wares added to the din.

Many of the stalls were selling eatables. Delicious aromas

The Tournament

floated in the air but the boys had no money and had to be content with only feasting their eyes and noses!

But some things were free. A puppet show, for instance, was being shown in an open stall. And then they saw a cock-fight. A number of men sat in a circle, each with well-fed roosters in bamboo cages. A man squatted in the middle of the circle, holding the biggest fowl they had ever seen. A basket near him brimmed over with bodies of dead roosters, victims of this powerful bird.

The man constantly taunted the others, challenging them to put up a cock against his champion. Suddenly one man, unable to take the boasts, dipped into his cage and brought out a cock, a fine bird with many coloured plumage and sharp beak and claws.

He placed his bird in front of the champion, whispered a few words of encouragement, and let go of the cock. Hackles raised, feathers glistening in the sun, the two cocks sprang into the fray. The spectators cheered the challenger on, urging him to teach the champion a lesson.

Alas, all in vain. The champion's claws suddenly flashed and sank deep into the challenger's throat. The bird fell onto the ground, thrashing its legs. The spectators let out a collective sigh. The champion's owner grinned broadly, put the dead cock into his basket and began calling out again.

'We can't spend the whole day here. Come, let's head for the tournament ground,' urged Govinda.

'Whew!' exclaimed Gopal as they neared the arena, his eyes round with wonder. 'I never imagined so many people

The Boy who became King

lived on this earth. There must be thousands and thousands of people here!'

The arena was rectangular, enclosed on all sides by a strong bamboo fencing. The only entry was from the eastern end, where there was a wide wooden gate over which officials and armed soldiers kept guard.

At the southern side, slightly away from the barricade, two tall, bamboo platforms had been erected. A ladder was provided to go up, and another to go down on the other side.

'What are those?' Sureng asked Govinda.

'They are the platforms from which the nobility will watch the games. One is for the king, his queen, the principle ministers and their families. The other is for the nobles and their families.'

But for a quirk of fate, Govinda thought to himself, you would have been sitting there today!

'Where do we sit?' Gopal, who had not got over his shock at seeing such a vast crowd, asked in a small voice.

'There,' said Govinda, pointing to the galleries on the north and west. The three boys pushed their way through the crowd and succeeded in finding seats in the west gallery.

Two drummers now entered the arena. Beating their drums they announced the arrival of the ministers and other court functionaries. A sudden hush fell on the crowd, and all eyes turned towards the bamboo platforms.

The nobles arrived in full regalia, atop caparisoned elephants. A band, playing drums, buffalo-horn flutes and other such instruments, welcomed them. The mahouts

The Tournament

stopped the elephants beside the platforms and the nobles and their families climbed directly onto the platforms and took their designated seats.

On the royal platform two chairs remained vacant. This was a reminder to the people that the throne at Charaideo was unoccupied.

The Buragohain and the Bargohain waved to the spectators. The people cheered and waved back. Then the Buragohain signalled for the games to begin.

Sureng and Gopal looked around them. Every inch of sitting space was occupied. Women and children were present in great numbers. Many people, not finding room in the galleries, had climbed up trees in the adjoining area. Excitement filled the air.

The heralds beat a long tattoo on their drums and announced that the first item was an aerial competition involving trained falcons. Half a dozen falcon-trainers ran into the arena, with birds chained to their arms. The eyes of the fierce-looking falcons were covered with cloth hoods. The trainers bowed to the ministers and took up their positions. Assistants carried cages filled with game-birds.

The Buragohain signalled again and the assistants released the captive birds. Moments later the trainers unleashed the falcons, took off their hoods and set them after the fleeing game-birds.

The falcons soared up and were soon mere specks against the cloudless, azure sky.

All eyes were turned towards the aerial fights high up.

The Boy who became King

One of the specks grew bigger and bigger and soon a falcon glided down gracefully, a dead bird in its talons. After depositing the bundle of feathers on the cloth spread by its master, it soared up again in pursuit of another kill.

A roar of appreciation erupted from the galleries. The cheering grew louder as other falcons appeared with their victims. The piles of dead bodies on the sheets of cloth grew bigger and bigger.

Half an hour later the contest came to an end. Five of the falcons returned to their owners. They cleaned their blood-stained beaks and hooded them. The unfortunate trainer whose bird had failed to return trembled at the thought of the punishment which would be meted out to him.

After count had been taken of the number of game-birds killed by each falcon, the trainer with the greatest number of kills was declared winner. The proud man ascended the steps of the platform and was rewarded with a gold necklace by the Buragohain. The crowd clapped enthusiastically. But the cheers turned to hoots and jeers as the luckless trainer whose bird had failed to return was tied to a whipping-post and given ten lashes.

The next item on the programme was announced—a fight between two elephants, a spectacular sport fraught with great risk. Soldiers armed with spears stationed themselves at various points along the outer side of the barricade. On several occasions in the past a fighting elephant had broken the barrier and charged the spectators, killing and injuring many. The soldiers were there to drive away a beast when it came too close to the fencing.

The Tournament

To the sound of drumbeats two mammoth tuskers entered through the gate. The animals were covered with ropes, a brass bell hung around the neck of each beast. They had been fed on hemp weeds and as a result were extremely unruly. The mahouts upon their backs had a tough time controlling them. The entry gate was left open.

The two antagonists, long, pointed tusks gleaming in the sunshine, stood confronting each other at the two ends of the arena. Then, prodded by their mahouts, they charged.

The crowd held its breath. No one moved. No one uttered a word. Pin drop silence reigned.

The two animals clashed headlong. There were terrible, loud thuds as they battled each other, using their heads, trunks and tusks. The mahouts lay flat upon the elephants' broad backs, clinging on to the ropes for dear life.

The beasts broke out of a clinch and retreated a few paces. The mahouts sat up and poked them with iron spikes. Raising their trunks and uttering blood-curdling trumpets, the enraged beasts charged again.

Moments before the collision one of the elephants, guided by its mahout, slowed down and wheeled quickly to the left. The other beast, carried forward by its own momentum found itself at a disadvantage, having presented its hind side to its opponent. The other elephant was quick to seize the opportunity. It moved swiftly, intent on burying its deadly tusks into the other's flank.

The spectators tensed, wondering whether this would be the end of the combat. But the second tusker made an almost impossible turn and swerved quickly away just as its opponent lunged at it. The sharp tips of the tusks, rather than sinking into its belly, simply grazed the skin. A fine trickle of blood appeared on its hide.

The crowd erupted into cheers. They jumped up and down, shouting and gesticulating in excitement and appreciation. Gopal cringed, but Sureng applauded as lustily as the others.

The beasts broke apart once again and circled each other from a distance.

'Fight, fight!' chanted the crowd.

'Kill, Kill!' they screamed.

Again and again the elephants charged, tusks and trunks repeatedly locking. All of a sudden there was a mighty, cracking sound and the audience gasped. The tusk of one elephant had broken into two. Trumpeting in pain and terror, the animal retreated.

Finding itself having the upper hand, the other pressed home its advantage. The mahout on top of the injured beast tried to make it face the assault head on. But the beast obviously had had enough and was looking for a way of escape.

Then to everyone's utter horror the injured elephant angered by the mahout's attempts to keep it in the fray suddenly reared up and came heavily down. The man on its back, caught unawares, toppled onto the ground.

A horrible scream emerged from his throat as the animal placed a foreleg on his body, smashing him to pulp. Then the animal loped out of the arena, pursued by its victorious opponent. The spectators were stunned. They gazed in

The Tournament

terror as assistants came rushing to the help of the fallen mahout. But he was dead. They picked up his body and carried it out.

Govinda was shaken to the core. He looked at the two other boys. The blood had drained from Gopal's face, but Sureng seemed unmoved by the tragedy.

'How awful!' Gopal muttered, speaking with difficulty.

'Serves him right,' was Sureng's comment. 'He made a mistake and that cost him his life.'

As if to ease the tension, a troupe of acrobats entered the arena. They were quaintly dressed indicating that they were not natives. They entertained the crowd by performing gymnastic feats and were warmly applauded.

A buffalo fight was next. Two huge animals were dragged into the arena. The men, having released the beasts, scampered across the barricade to safety. The animals stood a few yards apart, pawing the ground and snorting in challenge. Then they rushed at each other, using their heads as battering rams.

But all too soon one animal lost heart and ran away. The victor continued to trot around the arena to the cheers of the crowd.

Sureng was not too impressed by the archery display that followed. The archers shot at and hit moving targets. Sureng was certain he could equal their feat and do even better.

The drummers then announced the start of *Mal-Juj* or wrestling. Sureng sat up. This was what he had been waiting for.

The Boy who became King

A giant of a man entered the arena. The crowd gasped at the man's build. Almost six and a half feet tall, his muscular body naked except for a short dhoti, the wrestler looked formidable.

'This is the honourable Buragohain's fighter,' the drummers shouted at the top of their voices. 'Whoever succeeds in beating this champion will get whatever he demands. This is what the honourable Buragohain has declared, O good people.'

The spectators were agog with excitement. Sureng's eyes were fixed upon the huge wrestler. He was judging the man's strengths and weaknesses.

One by one opponents entered the arena to fight the Buragohain's champion. Three man were knocked out and limped out, accompanied by catcalls and booing. Then a fourth entered. He was the local favourite, a wrestler of repute. He was greeted with loud applause.

The two adversaries faced each other warily, looking for an opening. Suddenly the challenger sprang, caught the giant around his waist, and tried to trip him. But the man seemed to be made of rock. He put his palms flat on the other's shoulders and pressed hard.

The challenger shuddered with pain, went down on his knees and, fortunately for him was able to squirm out of the vice-like grip.

The giant laughed a full-throated laugh, beat his hands on his thighs, and pranced around the other wrestler. He looked more like a huge ape than a human being.

His wily opponent sprang at him again, head bent low,

The Tournament

trying to butt him in the belly. His head did hit the intended target, but had little impact. Before the man could retreat the giant's hands clamped around his waist, and squeezed.

The challenger could not move. He was totally paralysed. Blood rushed to his head. He hit out desperately with his fists, but the pain caused by the squeezing hands soon became unbearable, and his legs gave way. When, finally, the giant loosened his grip, the challenger fell down unconscious. He was dragged out of the arena by assistants.

The remaining wrestlers lost heart at the drubbing of the favourite. Some refused to take up the challenge, and the two who ventured into the arena, had to bite the dust.

The crowd gave the Buragohain's champion a big hand. He strutted about before the gathering, acknowledging the cheers. Sureng nudged Gopal and said, 'He's strong, but slow and heavy. He lacks technique. I've been watching him. He won by brute strength alone. I think I can bring him down.'

Govinda overheard him. 'Don't even think of it, Sureng,' he cautioned. 'Outsiders are not allowed into the arena. The soldiers will arrest you.'

'I'll take the risk,' Sureng retorted. And before anyone could stop him, he jumped off the gallery, climbed over the barricade and ran into the arena.

At first the spectators were too taken aback to react. But when they realized that the boy meant to fight the giant, there were murmurs of concern and pleas to return to the

The Boy who became King

gallery. Ignoring them, Sureng ran to the bottom of the platform and addressed the ministers.

'I seek your permission to fight this wrestler.'

The ministers and their entourage tittered. The Buragohain smiled tolerantly and said, 'Young man, I admire your courage. But I don't want a fine lad like you to be maimed for life. Go back to your parents. I'll overlook your misdemeanour in entering the arena without permission.'

'Does it mean you fear for the safety of your slave?' Sureng said insolently.

The smile was wiped off the minister's face. No one dared to speak to him in that tone, least of all a commoner and a young boy at that. He contained himself with an effort and said, 'Go then, boy. Fight him and be paid for your insolence.'

Sureng hitched up his dhoti and tied it firmly around his waist. Then he marched up to the wrestler and faced him boldly.

There was complete silence in the arena. No one was happy at the thought of the severe thrashing the youngster was certain to receive. Sureng was tall, but the giant was taller. Sureng seemed quite strong, but the giant was definitely stronger.

Though the crowd backed Sureng to a man, no one doubted what the final outcome would be. The wrestler glared at the boy and said contemptuously, 'You young upstart! Go back where you came from, or I'll squash you as I would a fly.'

The Tournament

'Try it, you over-fed ape,' Sureng retorted, carefully watching every move his opponent made.

The big man's lips curled into a snarl. That's it, Sureng thought to himself. Make him angry and he'll lose his sense of judgement. Then I'll be in control. Sureng had planned his tactics—the other wrestlers had made the mistake of rushing at the man. He, on the other hand, would move very little from his position, and wait for his opponent to come at him.

He must ensure that the giant rushed at him. The best way to achieve this would be to provoke him further. Sureng danced around his opponent, making him turn round and round, taunting him all the while. Suddenly Sureng lunged, feigned attack and then stepped deftly back. The giant's hands curled around empty air as he tried to catch Sureng.

Now the man was both angry and puzzled, astonished by the boy's agility. Sureng made as if to move to his right, then moved nimbly to the left. Stepping close, he lashed out with his foot and dealt the giant a painful blow on the shin.

The spectators shouted with delight. Whistles and catcalls rent the air. This infuriated the giant further. Muttering an oath, he rushed at Sureng.

This was the moment the boy had been waiting for. As the man came at him, he grasped one of his outstretched hands and pulled with all his might. Simultaneously he turned around so that his back was towards his opponent and bending low, using his body as a lever to upset the giant's balance, he abruptly straightened his body and, to the amazement of the crowd, the undefeated champion went flying through the air and landed heavily many yards away.

The galleries rose as one man. Such was the din that birds nesting in the nearby trees flew up in panic.

Sureng did not give his opponent a chance to recover. As the dazed man tottered to his feet, the boy's right hand went around his throat. He pulled the man's head back while kicking his feet from under him. Once again the giant fell heavily. He lay spread-eagled on the ground, making no further attempt to rise.

The crowd gave Sureng a tumultuous ovation. Waving at the spectators, the victor climbed up the platform and bowed before the principal ministers.

The Buragohain gave the boy a reluctant smile. 'You are a strong, brave and intelligent lad,' he said. 'What's your name? Where have you come from?'

'I'm Sureng from the village of Kalabari. I am the son of Surjya Bipra. Can I have my reward now?'

The Buragohain raised an eyebrow. A brahmin's son? The boy's name and appearance did not indicate it!

'We shall reward you amply,' he said. 'Ask what you wish for, and it will be yours.'

'I want to sit for a while on that throne,' Sureng said, pointing at the vacant royal throne. 'I wish to find out what it feels like to be a king.'

9

Escape

The Buragohain was stunned. He looked closely at the boy in front of him, to see if he was joking. But the handsome face before him was serious.

'Only the king is entitled to sit on that chair,' he replied with a frown. 'No one else may do so, even for a moment. Ask for something else.'

Sureng's face became haughty. Looking at him, the Buragohain was reminded of someone, but for the life of him he could not recollect who it was.

'You don't keep your promise,' the boy said arrogantly. 'I, Sureng, don't ask twice.'

He tossed his head imperiously and turned his back to the Buragohain. As he climbed down, the crowd believing that he had been rewarded, cheered him all the way across the arena, over the barricade and into the stands. Sureng sat down again with Govinda and Gopal.

The Boy who became King

The Buragohain was cut to the quick by the child's rebuff. But he was a man of principle. He admitted to himself that the boy was not at fault. It was he who was unable to keep his word. So, although Sureng's rebuff stung him, the idea of punishing the boy never entered his mind.

What a handsome lad! A commoner, and a rustic to boot! Yet his ways were regal. His words and actions were those of a king!

Suddenly something clicked in the Buragohain's mind. With a shock he realized who the boy had reminded him of. The late king, Tyaokhamti!

And those eyes! Surely they belonged to the defenceless but proud woman whom he had set adrift on a raft one dark night over fourteen years ago!

Was it possible that the Younger Queen had survived her ordeal? Was she alive, hiding in some village? Then why, after the death of Tyaokhamti and his queen had been announced, had she not come forward and brought her child to them?

The reason, of course, was obvious. She could trust no one. She had preferred having her son grow up as a commoner than reveal his identity and expose him to danger.

The Buragohain stood up and walked over to where the Bargohain sat on the other side of the vacant thrones.

'Did you notice that boy?' he asked in an urgent whisper.

'The one who knocked down your wrestler?'

'Yes. Did he not remind you of the late king?'

It was the Bargohain's turn to look surprised. 'You're right,' he said excitedly. 'I too was struck by the boy's looks.

Escape

Now that I think back, he bore a striking resemblance to Tyaokhamti.'

'The Younger Queen's child, eh? What do you think?'

'Didn't he introduce himself to you?'

'Yes, he did. Alas, if only I'd paid more attention. He even gave me the name of his village, but I can't remember it. All I remember is that he claimed to be the son of some Bipra or the other.'

'Why don't we find out? He might still be in the crowd. Send some soldiers to bring him here.'

The Buragohain immediately summoned the Captain of the Guards and gave him clear instructions.

'Go and fetch the boy who just won the wrestling bout. He should be in the galleries. If he resists, your soldiers must overpower him. But on no account is he to be hurt. If you as much as harm a hair on his head, you'll spend the rest of your days in a dungeon.'

The officer left hurriedly. In the stands people milled around Sureng eagerly. He was one of them and they savoured his victory as if it had been their own. Some embraced him warmly, others patted him on the back.

An old woman shuffled up to him and lovingly stroked his face. 'Son,' she asked, 'what did the Buragohain give you as reward?'

'Nothing,' replied Sureng shortly.

'Nothing,' people around him cried out in chorus.

'Yes, nothing! That old man up there asked me what I wanted. I replied that I wanted to sit on the empty throne for a moment to feel what it was like to be a king.'

The Boy who became King

A murmur broke out among the crowd. Dismay was writ large on every face.

'But don't you know that only a king can sit on that throne?' the old woman asked.

'That's what he told me. So I accused him of not keeping his word, turned my back on him and left.'

Everyone was aghast. They were very worried that Sureng, a commoner, had insulted the senior-most minister of the court.

'You have been foolish,' the old woman admonished. 'That was the Buragohain, the most powerful man in the kingdom. If you have offended him, he can have you killed.'

'It would be wise of you to leave at once,' another well-wisher urged Govinda.

'I thank you all for your concern. But rest easy. I have done no wrong. I would rather die than steal away like a coward,' said Sureng obstinately.

He sat back and continued to calmly watch the proceedings in the arena. The sun was now high overhead. The final item in the programme was about to begin. This was to be a fight between wild animals, a fitting climax to the morning's entertainment.

Govinda was greatly perturbed by the warnings of his fellow spectators. As if to prove them right, he saw through the corner of his eye a group of soldiers striding briskly across the open space that separated the galleries from the barricade. Every now and then the soldiers stopped to scan the faces of the spectators.

Escape

Others nearby saw them too. They renewed their appeals to Sureng. Their pleas fell on deaf ears. Unperturbed, Sureng continued to sit where he was.

Knowing Sureng well, Govinda changed his tactics and said, 'Think of your brother, Gopal. He will be captured with you. So will I. Who knows, the Buragohain might wreak vengeance on our family, if not the entire village.'

For the first time Sureng seemed to relent. 'Is that true?' he asked the old woman.

'Too true, too true,' replied the woman, vigorously nodding her head.

'Then let's go, brother,' said Sureng, springing up from his seat.

By now the soldiers were within a stone's throw of them. As the three lads rose to leave, the Captain of the Guards saw them and said something to his soldiers. The group began striding rapidly towards them.

'For heaven's sake, do something!' Govinda told those around him. 'Create a commotion, start a fracas!'

The crowd was quick to respond. Those near them abruptly stood up and cheered. Their eyes were fixed on the cages in which two animals were engaged in a fight unto death. Many of them jumped from the galleries and ran up to the barricade wall. Those farther away, eager to learn of the cause of the commotion, pressed forward. The soldiers were caught in the melee and lost sight of their quarry.

Govinda, Gopal and Sureng slipped away in the confusion. When order was finally restored in the stands, they

The Boy who became King

were nowhere in sight. The Captain of the Guards rushed to report to the Buragohain. The minister was furious.

'Do you value your life, officer?' he thundered.

'Yes,' stammered the frightened fellow.

'Then go and alert every soldier in the city. We must not lose trace of that boy. Proclaim a reward of a hundred gold coins for his capture. But, I repeat, he must not be harmed in any way.'

'There's one lead we can follow,' said the Bargohain. 'The boy must have come by boat from his village.'

'Good thinking,' said the Buragohain approvingly. 'Officer, send some soldiers to the ghat where visiting boats are moored. Ask them to look out for a tall, handsome boy.'

The officer hastened to do as he had been ordered. A posse of soldiers immediately set out for the landing-ghat.

Meanwhile, Govinda and his companions had left the tournament site unseen. They moved quickly across the fair-ground. As most of the people had gone to the tournament, there were very few people at the fair. Sureng would have dearly loved to linger and go round the stalls, but every wasted moment was fraught with danger. They hurried past the beckoning stalls.

'We seem to have raised a hornet's nest,' Govinda said. Sureng grinned impishly, but the very next moment his face became serious. A company of soldiers was coming towards them from the opposite direction. The trio slowed down to a walking pace so as not to arouse suspicion. The soldiers looked at them disinterestedly and marched by.

Escape

This made them complacent. Convinced that they had escaped detection they walked on briskly enough, but not as quickly as before. As they reached the end of the dirt-track and were about to enter the outskirts of the city of Charaideo, they saw the same group of soldiers—now behind them. But this time the armed soldiers were coming at a fast trot.

The soldiers started shouting when they sighted the three boys. Sureng and Govinda could have out-run their pursuers, but not little Gopal. The only way of escape was to throw them off the trail.

They rushed into Charaideo's tree-lined avenues. Not many people were about: the citizens had gone off to the tournament. Govinda led them off the main street into a by-lane. They hid behind a clump of bushes beside a little cottage, and waited for the soldiers to pass.

They heard the tread of heavy feet as the soldiers raced by, and heaved breaths of relief. But the relief was short lived. The door of the cottage opened and a housemaid, carrying an earthen pot at her waist, came out. She was on her way to the community pond to fill water.

She saw them crouching behind the bushes. Though not of great intelligence, yet even she could reason that three people hiding in such a manner could not be up to any good.

'Daylight robbers!' she thought. 'Help, help!' she shrieked at the top of her voice. 'Robbers! Cut-throats! Help, help!' The pot dropped from her hand and shattered.

Govinda folded his hands and pleaded with his eyes. But the more he pleaded, the louder grew her screams.

The Boy who became King

The soldiers heard her and turned back. The three knew they had to leave their hiding place and leave quickly! Govinda led the boys into a maze of alleys and by-lanes.

When they caught up with the distraught girl, the soldiers asked her why she was yelling her head off. 'Daylight robbers!' she said, continuing to scream though the men were near. 'I saw them. Vicious characters, armed to the teeth.'

'How many?'

'Must have been a dozen,' the girl shrieked, enjoying herself hugely. There had never been such excitement in the life of drudgery that she led.

'They went that way,' she continued, pointing in the direction the trio had taken.

'Take care,' she yelled. 'They're desperate men!'

The soldiers went off in the indicated direction. The girl's eyes glowed with excitement. Ah, the fun she would have, retelling this experience at washing time! She would, of course, embroider her tale to make it more thrilling.

In the meantime Govinda led the boys through the streets, halting every now and again to ensure that their way was clear. Unseen dangers could be lurking behind every corner. More soldiers had joined the first group.

As the boys turned a sharp bend, they almost collided with a group of soldiers. The soldiers immediately gave chase. The three ran back the way they had come. To their dismay they found their way blocked by another set of soldiers.

They were trapped. There seemed to be no way out. In

Escape

desperation Govinda jumped across a bamboo fence that enclosed the large compound of a fine-looking house. Sureng and Gopal followed.

Fortunately there was no one in the house. Going around the house, the soldiers hot on their heels, they came to a large cowshed in the backyard, and ran inside.

The cowshed was empty. The cattle must have been sent out to graze. A loft high up was filled with stacks of hay. A bamboo ladder led to the loft.

The shed smelt strongly of cow dung, but this was no time to be finicky. They climbed up to the loft, pulled up the ladder along with them and placed it so that it was not visible from below. Then they covered themselves with the hay.

And not a moment too soon! As they waited with bated breath, they heard the footsteps of the soldiers rushing into the cowshed. But the missing ladder fooled them. Not suspecting that anyone was in the loft, the soldiers gave a cursory glance around the empty shed and rushed out again.

After over an hour in the cowshed, the three lads emerged and dusted themselves to remove the strands of hay sticking to their clothes and hair. The coast seemed clear. They climbed over the fence and set off for the ghat.

Surprisingly, they met no soldiers on the way. The search for them must have been called off. It was late afternoon when they crossed the city and reached the path leading to the ghat.

Here too they encountered no soldiers. But, once bitten,

The Boy who became King

they were twice shy, and proceeded with extreme caution. Just as well for, on reaching the river, they found the place guarded by a score of armed troops.

Many who had come for the tournament had already left, so the river at that point was not as crowded with boats as before. The soldiers were diligently checking everyone who was leaving. There was not the ghost of a chance that they could reach their craft without being seen.

'Now what?' Govinda asked, more to himself than the others. But Sureng remained undaunted.

'I'll show myself to them,' he said, 'and draw them away from the boat. You seize the chance and get aboard.'

'But we can't leave you behind!' Gopal exclaimed.

'Of course not. Row downstream and wait for me some distance away. I'll join you as quickly as I can.'

Before Govinda could argue with him, Sureng was on his way. He sprinted down the track, slowing to a walk as he neared the bank. A guard saw him, and raised the alarm. Sureng started as if surprised, turned left and bolted along the bank.

The soldiers raced after him. Govinda and Gopal did not linger. They ran to their boat and rowed swiftly away. So intent were the soldiers on catching Sureng that they did not see them leave.

Sureng drew the soldiers far away from the boats. Then suddenly he turned right, intending to dive into the river. Just then a soldier pulled out a short piece of rope with two stones attached to the end from his waist. Expertly

Escape

swinging the rope in the air, he flung it at Sureng. It curled around the boy's legs and brought him down.

The boy fell heavily. He recovered quickly and untangled the rope from his ankles. But not quickly enough. Before he could reach the safety of the waters, soldiers surrounded him, their swords drawn.

Others might have surrendered in such a situation, but not Sureng. He raised his fists and faced the soldiers. The guards could have easily cut him down but they had been instructed to bring the boy alive and unharmed. Moreover, having seen his prowess against a reputed wrestler, the soldiers hesitated approaching him without their swords.

As they stood undecided about their next move, 'Put down your swords, you idiots!' their leader barked out. Sureng could not believe his ears. He stared in astonishment as the soldiers sheathed their weapons.

So the Buragohain wanted him alive! Not if he could help it. He flexed his knees as the men lunged at him. A deep growl, like that of a wild animal, emerged from his throat. He caught hold of a soldier, lifted him bodily, and flung him at the others. They fell back, overawed by the ferocity of his attack.

Sureng dived into the river.

A few soldiers dived in after him, others raced towards the boats. Their eyes scanned the surface of the water as they waited for Sureng to emerge. To their amazement, there was no sign of the boy.

Half a mile downstream Govinda and Gopal waited

The Boy who became King

anxiously. All of a sudden there was a ripple and Sureng popped up beside their boat.

He chuckled at their astonished faces. 'I've been swimming underwater for most of the distance,' he said. 'Let's not waste time. The soldiers are right behind us.'

They set off at full tilt. The downstream current helped them gather speed. They soon left their pursuers far behind.

As they did not linger and took turns at the oars, they completed the return journey in half the time it had taken them earlier. Only Surjya Bipra and Dhinai were told of their narrow escape. Though Gopal and Sureng enthralled the village youngsters with descriptions of the tournament, they did not mention Sureng's exploits.

A few weeks later a passing boatman brought grave news. The principle ministers of the court had announced a reward of one hundred gold coins to anyone who could give information about a mysterious boy who had beaten the Buragohain's wrestler in the tournament. Everyone thought that the minister wanted to punish the boy for having insulted him, though the proclamation did not say this.

Surjya Bipra and the others did not know that the Buragohain's reasons for seeking Sureng were quite different!

10

The Brahmin Prince

Thaokhuncheng was a prosperous merchant from Charaideo. An enterprising fellow, there was no commodity that he did not buy or sell. But he traded mostly in cattle, purchasing them cheaply from far-flung villages and selling them at a higher price at the cattle-market near Charaideo.

This time his trip was exclusively to buy cattle. This was the first time he was setting foot in the village of Kalabari.

It was the rainy season and the Lohit was overflowing. The currents were treacherous, making travel by boat risky. The astute merchant, however, knew that the risks were worth taking. The monsoon brought with it disease and death, both for men and animals. So the villagers were eager to sell off their surplus cattle at whatever price they were offered.

The Boy who became King

He was travelling in a trading boat. Six able-bodied men were required to guide the craft.

Being rich, Thaokhuncheng had plenty of gold and silver, but the villagers preferred salt, trinkets, scented wood and similar items in exchange for their cattle. So the trader carried a large amount of these items in his boat.

The scene before him, as he neared the bank, was typical of rural life in those parts. Women were washing clothes on the bank, men were in the fields. Children frolicked in the water close to the bank. At a distance a cowherd could be heard playing a melancholy melody on a bamboo flute. The atmosphere was calm and peaceful.

The merchant's arrival disturbed the placidity. When he disembarked, a crowd of naked children, inquisitive-eyed, wet bodies glistening in the sun, immediately surrounded him. The women too threw him curious glances. He secured their approval by distributing chunks of molasses among the children.

He marched into the village with a boisterous group of children following at his heels. On the way he saw some youths engaged in a game of *Dhopkhel*. The merchant was about to pass on when his gaze fell upon one of the players.

He stopped dead in his tracks. Pretending to be interested in the game, he observed the boy closely. His heart began to beat furiously. Possessing a good memory for faces, there was no doubt in his mind. The tall, sturdy boy was the same one he had seen in the tournament at Charaideo!

The merchant's mind began to race. A purse of a hundred

The Brahmin Prince

gold coins had been offered for information about this boy. That was no small fortune!

'Who is that tall youth? The one with the *dhop*?'

'Oh, that's Sureng, the brahmin's son,' a child replied.

'Ah! A brahmin's son, is he? Did he go to Charaideo a few months back?'

'Oh, yes. Gopal went with him. They had a wonderful time at the tournament. Told us all about it.'

The merchant gave the youngster a large chunk of molasses, while silently congratulating himself. Being a man without moral principles, Thaokhuncheng was not concerned about why the Buragohain sought the boy. He thought only in terms of profit and loss. All he cared about was that the lad was worth a hundred gold coins!

On no account must he let this opportunity slip through his fingers, he thought to himself. He would cut short his trip and return to Charaideo as soon as possible. But before that he had to find out more about Sureng.

So, towards the latter part of the day, after the haggling was over and some transactions had been done, he cautiously enquired about the boy. The replies of the unsuspecting villagers did not give him much information. But he did learn two vital facts. Sureng was not Surjya Bipra's real son, but had been adopted. Also, no one in the village had seen his mother when she was alive.

That very evening, having put the cattle on board, Thaokhuncheng set off for Charaideo.

The Boy who became King

The Buragohain was a worried man. The burden of running the kingdom without a king weighed heavily on him. He sat in the outer room of his mansion discussing the situation with the Bargohain.

'We have ruled eight years without a king,' he said. 'It is becoming more and more difficult to manage the affairs of the realm. A successor has to be found.'

The Bargohain nodded gravely. 'The nobles have begun complaining. They blame us for killing Tyaokhamti without thinking about a successor. The ordinary citizens too are restive.'

'That's the way of the world. The wheel always moves full circle. At that time they danced with joy and made heroes of us. Now the same people are calling us villains, if not to our faces, at least behind our backs.'

'The administration too is getting lax in the absence of a central authority.'

'That boy . . . if only we had found out where he came from! But, I suppose, it's my fault. I should have remembered what he told me.'

'You seem certain that he is the Younger Queen's child.'

'The more I think about it, the more certain I become. That face, those eyes! The way he walked and talked. I'm sure I'm not mistaken.'

At that moment a servant entered, bowed before the ministers and said, 'Your Excellencies, a man named Thaokhuncheng waits outside.'

'Who is he? What does he want?' the Buragohain asked in an irritated tone.

The Brahmin Prince

'A merchant, Your Excellency. He requests an audience.'

'Tell him to come later.'

'He claims to have news of the boy who was at the tournament.'

'What? Summon him at once.'

Moments later Thaokhuncheng entered. Even before he could kneel and bow to the ministers, the Buragohain asked, 'You have information about the boy?'

'Yes, Your Excellencies.'

'Scores of people have come with the same claim.'

'They were lying, tempted by hope of earning the reward,' the Bargohain added. 'They were whipped. So be careful that you speak the truth.'

'He is the boy you seek,' the merchant said confidently.

'Then speak up. Where is he?'

'The reward, Your Excellencies. The colour of gold is like oil . . . it loosens my tongue.'

'You are impertinent, indeed! I have half a mind to reward you by flinging you into a dungeon! My word is my bond. You will see your favourite colour only after we have checked your story.'

The merchant was unperturbed. 'His name is Sureng,' he said. 'Lives in a village called Kalabari.'

The name Sureng and Kalabari sounded familiar. The Buragohain was sure that these had been mentioned by the boy. But his face did not betray any emotion.

'Is he the son of a brahmin?'

'An adopted son, Your Excellency. The brahmin claims

The Boy who became King

that the boy is the son of his wife's sister. But nobody in the village ever saw the sister.'

The Buragohain leapt out of his chair. 'Come, Bargohain,' he urged, 'there's no time to lose. We must leave at once for this village. Merchant, you'll accompany us. If you're taking us on a wild goose chase, you'll live to regret it.'

Sureng sat in the shade of a banyan tree and played a melancholy tune on his flute. The music reflected his mood. Gopal sitting beside him said, 'You seem very sad, brother.'

Sureng put the flute away and placed an arm around his friend. 'You can't imagine how very sad I feel, Gopal. I have decided to leave Kalabari. The thought of leaving all of you makes my heart heavy.'

'Leave Kalabari? You can't do that!'

'I have to. You see, I'm no longer a child. I must think of the future. The older I grow, the more of a burden I'll be on our aged parents.'

Gopal's eyes filled with tears. 'They love you,' he said fervently. 'We all adore you. The talk of you being a burden is your own imagination.'

'No. Before we left for Charaideo, father talked to me about settling down. So did Govinda. They want me to take up a profession. But somehow, the idea of becoming a priest or a farmer seems too tame to me.'

'Then take me with you,' Gopal cried.

Before Sureng could reply a great commotion, coming

The Brahmin Prince

from the direction of the river, reached their ears. Moments later a friend of Sureng raced up to them.

'Come to the river-bank,' the boy shouted. 'You'll have never seen such a beautiful boat in your life!'

Sureng did not move. 'You go, Gopal. I'm in no mood to see boats, even beautiful ones. All I want to do is sit here and play my flute.'

Gopal also refused to go. He chose to remain with his friend. The other boy shrugged his shoulders and left. Picking up his flute, Sureng played another sad tune.

Others, however, were rushing towards the river-bank. The news of the approaching grand craft had spread like wildfire. Men, women and children dropped whatever they were doing and flocked to the river. They gazed awestruck as the royal barge sliced its way through the waters of the Lohit.

The barge shone like a jewel. It was a huge vessel. Rows of oarsmen pulled together at the oars. The boat-head was in the shape of a peacock, plated with gold and encrusted with precious gems. The polished woodwork glinted in the sunlight.

Govinda was taking a class when the news of the approaching vessel reached him. His blood ran cold. Dismissing his students, he ran into his house. Surjya Bipra was in the prayer-room, doing puja.

'We are in trouble, father!' he cried. 'The royal barge is approaching our village. The ministers are probably on it. They have come for Sureng.'

Overhearing him the brahmin's wife began sobbing as

The Boy who became King

though her heart would break. Surjya Bipra prostrated himself before the altar and beseeched the deities to come to their aid. He picked up the royal ring from under the altar, and left with Govinda to tell Dhinai the news.

Bashu, who too was at the workshop, broke down and cried. But his father said, 'Control yourself, son. It's now up to us to ensure Sureng's safety, even at the cost of our own lives.'

By the time they reached the bank, the entire village was gathered there. Surjya Bipra looked at the swiftly-moving barge and hope suddenly flooded his heart.

'Look,' he whispered to his companions. 'The principle ministers are on the barge, but only a few soldiers are with them. Had their intentions been hostile, boat-loads of soldiers would have followed.'

His words made the others optimistic. Perhaps he was right. The old brahmin clutched the ring tightly in his palm and muttered a prayer.

The barge pulled up at the ghat. Boatmen scrambled down to secure it with ropes. A gangway was lowered and the two ministers, followed by lesser functionaries and soldiers, crossed over to the bank. Thaokhuncheng came last, a smug smile playing on his lips.

The villagers, as one, prostrated themselves, foreheads touching the ground. The Buragohain asked them to rise.

'Who, among you, is the village brahmin?' he demanded authoritatively. 'We wish to speak to him.'

Surjya Bipra noted that the minister did not seem to be angry. He stepped up and said with dignity, 'I am Surjya

The Brahmin Prince

Bipra, the village priest. Have I offended you in any way, My Lord?'

The Buragohain smiled. 'No, old man, not at all,' he said. 'A few answers is all we seek of you. Come here to one side so we can speak in private.'

The villagers began to murmur among themselves, wondering what business the highest dignitaries of the land could have with a poor brahmin. The children gaped in wonder at the golden barge and the armed soldiers.

'You have a son named Sureng?' the Buragohain enquired.

'Yes, My Lord,' said the brahmin, determined not to give away more information than he was asked.

'He is not really your son, is he?'

'No, My Lord.'

The Buragohain saw through Surjya Bipra's tactic. 'I understand why you hesitate to give us information,' he said gently. 'You must not misunderstand our motive. If Sureng is indeed the boy we seek, you will be doing the country a great service.'

Surjya Bipra relaxed. The destined moment had arrived. The secret that had been so carefully guarded must now be revealed. It was the will of Providence. He was merely an instrument in the hands of God.

The words came tumbling out. He narrated how they had found the Younger Queen drifting on a raft and had brought her home. Sureng was that unfortunate queen's son. It was necessary, he explained, to keep the facts hidden, for they had feared for the young child's safety.

The Boy who became King

'Do you have any proof that you are telling the truth?'

The brahmin opened his palm and handed over the royal ring. The Buragohain examined it closely and passed it on to the Bargohain. The two nodded at each other. The crowd waited with bated breath.

So elated was the Buragohain that he embraced the brahmin. The villagers, emboldened at this, began to cheer. The Buragohain raised his hands for silence.

'The king has been found,' he proclaimed loudly. 'Long live the king.'

The villagers picked up the refrain and the village of Kalabari resounded with their cries. The noise reached Sureng and Gopal. They wondered what the noise was all about.

Suddenly Gopal gaped, caught Sureng by the shoulders, and pointed. The sight startled Sureng too.

A big crowd was coming towards them. Sureng recognized the two people leading the procession—the ministers he had met at the tournament. But, wonder of wonders, Surjya Bipra was walking alongside them! And the entire village seemed to be following.

The procession came right up to the stunned boys. What happened next was even stranger. The nobles and their retinues knelt before Sureng. He looked on open-mouthed as everyone, including his parents, brothers and friends, prostrated themselves before him.

Little Gopal, seeing that everyone else was kneeling, was about to follow suit, but Sureng restrained him.

The Brahmin Prince

'We salute Your Majesty,' the Buragohain said loudly. 'Please permit us to rise.'

'Why do you mock me by addressing me as Your Majesty?' Sureng cried. 'Father . . . mother . . . tell them I'm your son.'

At a signal from the Buragohain everyone rose. Overwhelmed with emotion Surjya Bipra remained silent.

'No, Your Highness,' the Bargohain said. 'You are not a brahmin's son. You are the son of King Tyaokhamti, and heir to the Ahom throne.'

Sureng's familiar world began to crumble. Bewildered, he turned to Surjya Bipra for reassurance. 'Father, this isn't true, is it?'

'Yes, Your Majesty,' the priest replied in a tear-choked voice. 'You are the son of King Tyaokhamti. I gave shelter to your mother, the Younger Queen. Before she died she left you in my care.'

Sureng's eyes grew moist. Even his revered father had addressed him in a formal fashion. Nothing was the same any more. He wanted to cry, but his fierce pride would not allow the tears to flow.

'You will be told the whole story,' promised the Buragohain. 'But now you must leave this village and go to Charaideo, where we will proclaim you king.'

'No, no,' Sureng's voice was strong again. 'I won't leave Kalabari. I won't leave my parents and brothers.'

The two ministers looked at each other. Then the Buragohain said, 'Surjya Bipra and his family can come with you to Charaideo. We owe him much for having brought you up and looked after you so well.'

The Boy who became King

Sureng's eyes probed the faces of the villagers. They gazed at him in awe, as if they understood and feared the enormous power he now wielded. There now seemed to be a great wall even between himself and his closest friends, with whom he had played and hunted and shared so many exciting adventures. Nothing would be the same again!

Sureng shook his head as if to shake off the conflict and confusion in his mind. 'Come,' he said. 'What must be, must be. If I am the king, then to Charaideo I shall have to go.'

When the royal barge left Kalabari the entire village was present at the bank to see Sureng off. Tears flowed from every eye. But they were tears of happiness, not sorrow.

Surjya Bipra stayed back with his family to wind up his affairs. Sureng promised to send for them within a fortnight. He stood at the vessel's stern and waved to his former companions. He had heard the story of his birth from his foster father. The treatment his father and the Elder Queen had meted out to his mother filled him with anger.

I shall not ascend the throne at Charaideo, he silently resolved. I shall select another site as my capital, take the name of Sudangpha and rule the country wisely.

The village disappeared from view. With a final wave of his hand the Brahmin Prince turned his back on the past, and prepared himself to face a totally different future.